**'You know you're beautiful, Honey, and that makes you dangerous to be around.'**

She itched to lean forward, to close the distance between them, to throw her arms about his neck, to urge his head down so their lips could make contact. But she'd already sensed Edward was an old-fashioned type of man. She could nudge him a little, but if she went too far, too soon, she'd scare him off for good—and that was the last thing she wanted.

Slow and steady. She stayed where she was, but angled her head slightly, her hair sliding off her shoulder to reveal her neck. She watched as Edward's gaze dipped momentarily to the smooth skin, his pupils dilating for a fraction of a second, indicating he liked what he saw. It made her feel all warm and fuzzy inside.

'Dangerous for whom?'

**Lucy Clark** is actually a husband-and-wife writing team. They enjoy taking holidays with their children, during which they discuss and develop new ideas for their books using the fantastic Australian scenery. They use their daily walks to talk over characterisation and fine details of the wonderful stories they produce, and are avid movie buffs. They live on the edge of a popular wine district in South Australia with their two children, and enjoy spending family time together at weekends.

*The Boss She Can't Resist*
is Lucy Clark's 50th book
for Mills & Boon® Medical™ Romance!

# THE BOSS
# SHE CAN'T RESIST

BY
LUCY CLARK

First published in Great Britain 2012
by Mills & Boon, an imprint of Harlequin (UK) Limited.
Harlequin (UK) Limited, Eton House, 18-24 Paradise Road,
Richmond, Surrey TW9 1SR

© Anne Clark & Peter Clark  2012

ISBN: 978 0 263 22855 7

To Melanie & Austin—
you make our life easy...most days!

With love always, Mum & Dad

1 *Tim* 4:12

# CHAPTER ONE

HONEY changed gear, slowing the hot-pink car as she neared the outskirts of Oodnaminaby, the sub-alpine town where she would be spending the next twelve months of her life. It was through her friends Peter and Annabelle that she'd been fortunate enough to gain employment in the Oodnaminaby GP practice while Dr Lorelai Rainbow went on maternity leave.

Honey had a good feeling about this town. She'd worked in several towns over the years, searching, yearning for the place where she might feel at home. 'Oodnaminaby.' She spoke the name of the town out loud. 'Hello, I'm Dr Huntington-Smythe and I live in Oodnaminaby.' She smiled and shook her head at her own folly. 'One day, Honey. You'll find the place where you fit and the place that fits you.'

Here, in Oodnaminaby, she would be working with Peter's brother, a man she'd never met before but one she knew Peter held in high esteem. Her job interview had been conducted over several phone calls with Lorelai, the two women immediately bonding and becoming firm friends.

'I told Edward not to worry,' Lorelai had said two days ago, just before Honey had set out to drive from

Queensland to New South Wales. 'I told him I'd found the best replacement ever.'

'Is it me?' Honey had joked, and Lorelai had laughed down the line.

'I can't wait to meet you face to face— Oh, and thanks for the herbal tea you sent me. It's really helped my indigestion.'

'It makes my heart sing to hear that. I'll be there soon enough to take over so you, sweet Lorelai, can really rest because I've heard that growing a baby can be quite exhausting.'

Lorelai had laughed once more and soon their conversation had ended. Honey smiled at the memory and her hope that Oodnaminaby would be *the* place for her increased. She picked up the piece of paper that was on the seat next to her and glanced at the name of Peter's brother. '"Edward",' she read out loud. She was looking forward to meeting him, too. Peter had often spoken of his family. He had five brothers and Edward was the eldest—Honey had often found herself completely muddled as to who was who in the Goldmark family.

'"Edward Goldmark. Oodnaminaby Family Medical Practice, Lampe Street, Oodnaminaby,"' she read, before looking out the front windscreen searching for street names. She couldn't see any surgery and the houses she was passing had no numbers. When she saw an old weather-beaten sign that said Shops, she pulled into the parking lot. There were steps leading up to a brick colonnade sheltering a row of shops and right in front of her at the top of the steps was a clean glass window with the words Doctors' Surgery. She switched off the engine.

'I'm here.' She couldn't resist smiling as she unclipped her seat belt and opened the car door, stepping out into the crisp March morning. 'I'm here!' The words were louder, her tone filled with renewed energy and excitement as she quickly stretched her arms overhead before heading up the steps. The last two towns she'd worked in had felt promising to begin with but over time she'd found too many obstacles, both literally and figuratively, to stop her from settling down.

For most of her life, she'd been searching for the place where she belonged in this world. Being raised in what many people would call a 'hippy commune', she'd often found herself dissatisfied with life. At eighteen she'd left the commune, changed her name and continued looking for her mental, spiritual and emotional home. She'd been looking ever since.

Breathing in, her senses were tantalised by the fresh scent of sweet blossoms from native trees and surrounding shrubs. 'Glorious,' she pronounced. There didn't seem to be any sign of life this early and as she turned and looked at the scenic view of mountains, trees and a crystal-clear lake, she couldn't contain her joy. It was picture perfect.

Stretching both her arms out wide, her face tilted towards the sun, she spun in circles, her long purple skirt fanning out wide as she twirled.

'This. Place. Is. Gorgeous!' Honey punctuated each word as she continued to whirl around, breathing in the freedom of the morning.

'Can I help you?' A deep male voice spoke from behind her and Honey stopped spinning so suddenly, one of her multicoloured hair braids flicked her in the face. Wrinkling her nose, and a little disoriented from spinning, she realised she was still facing the wrong way. Turning quickly, she found a stern man standing with his feet planted firmly just outside the door to the surgery. He was dressed in navy trousers and a navy polo shirt, the top button undone.

'Oh. Hi.' Honey felt a tad self-conscious at being caught twirling but quickly swallowed it.

'What are you doing?' the man asked.

Honey's smile increased as she momentarily considered explaining the way majestic views, such as the one spread before them, made her feel. However, she'd discovered over the years that a lot of people didn't understand her connection to nature so she'd stopped trying to explain it.

'Twirling,' she offered, and smiled brightly, lifting her sunglasses to rest on the top of her head. The man before her was tall, dark, handsome and scowling, his arms crossed defensively over his firm chest, his dark brown eyes shuttered. 'This place is amazing.' Her smile was still bright as she spread her arms once more to encompass the view surrounding them. 'The mountain air just infuses your body and zaps it to life, doesn't it? Fantastic!'

'Is there something I can help you with?' Impatience had crept into his tone.

'Yes.' She faced him again, taking her sunglasses off her head and running her free hand through her long multicoloured hair. 'You can tell me how on earth anyone gets any work done when you're faced with such stunning views each morning?' She held out her hand. 'I'm Honey.'

The man gave one long blink as though he couldn't quite believe what he was hearing. '*You're* Honey?'

'Last time I checked,' she replied cheerfully. 'And you must be Eddie.'

'Edward,' he instantly corrected.

'Sorry. Edward,' she repeated, then looked closer at him. 'The family resemblance is certainly very strong. You and Peter could be the twins rather than Peter and Bart.'

Edward nodded. It wasn't the first time he'd heard that.

Being the eldest of five boys, though, they were all bound to resemble each other in some small way. He stepped forward and placed his hand in hers, accepting her polite greeting, even though he wanted to tell her to turn right around and head back to whatever carnival she'd sprung from. She looked so different from any doctor he'd ever met that he had to wonder whether his brother was playing a practical joke.

With her slim hand enclosed in his, Edward couldn't help but be aware of the oddest tingling sensation. So soft, so delicate, and his frown deepened before he quickly released his hold and folded his arms back across his chest. He stared at her again, as though not quite sure exactly what he was seeing. His new locum was dressed in a sleeveless orange top that buttoned down the front, a long, flowing purple skirt that swirled down to her ankles and her feet were strapped into a sort of flat leather sandal. Her hair was long and honey blonde in colour, except for the parts that were streaked purple, blue, red, green and pink. Her eyes… He squinted in the sun and almost leaned forward, trying to figure out exactly what colour they were before finally deciding that they were indeed a rich, deep blue, although sometimes in the light they looked almost violet.

When his business partner for the last six years, Lorelai Rainbow, had told him she would be taking twelve months off for maternity leave, he'd been more than happy for her. Although Lorelai had agreed to fill in for the odd clinic here and there, Edward had realised he'd need to find a locum. However, Lorelai had beaten him to the punch.

'Your brother Peter knows a doctor who's free to fill in for the year,' Lorelai had told him. 'I've read her résumé and I have to say it's highly impressive. I've also spoken to her on the phone several times and she sounds great.

We hit it off right away. Her name is Honey and she's just perfect for this position. I've completed all the paperwork, Ginny's filed it. It's a done deal. No need for you to worry.' Lorelai had patted him on the shoulder. 'I'd never leave you in the lurch so relax, Edward. It's all taken care of. Trust me.'

And he did. He trusted Lorelai implicitly both in business and personal matters but he'd known Lorelai for most of his life and considered her part of his family. Edward also trusted Peter's judgement, knowing his brother would never do anything to upset the family medical practice, which was their parents' legacy. Staring in stunned disbelief at the woman before him, he couldn't help but think that both Lorelai and Peter had had rocks in their heads at such a ludicrous recommendation.

This Honey woman was completely unsuitable for the traditional family general practice his parents had started over thirty years ago. The majority of people living in Oodnaminaby and surrounding districts, who had lived in the area for most of their lives, were very set in their ways and didn't take well to change.

'So…Edward. Would you like to give me a tour of the place?' Honey glanced around at the shops, rubbing her hands together, desperate to ignore the way her fingers had tingled as soon as they'd touched his. She may be searching for a home, a place where she felt she truly belonged, but she was most definitely not searching for any type of romantic entanglement.

'Or is this it?' She pointed to the general store, which, from the display in the windows, seemed to cover everything from groceries to clothes to pharmaceuticals. Next to it was a hot-food take-away shop, then a post office and a ski-hire/fishing-tackle shop.

'Uh…this is basically it.' He was still frowning, still

highly unsure of this strange but vibrant woman who stood before him. He watched as she walked—no, not walked, *glided*—a few steps away from where he stood, momentarily mesmerised by the gentle swish of her hips, the swirl of her skirt around her ankles, the way she rubbed her brown bare arms as the crispness of the morning started to raise goose-bumps on her skin.

'Not that there's anything wrong with all of this being "it",' she clarified, her voice as smooth as…well…honey. 'I like small towns. They form a tight-knit community where you can always rely on having a good ol' chinwag with your neighbour over the back fence. Ooh, look.' She took a step closer to the door of the medical clinic. 'You have brass plaques.' She quickly read them, reaching out to run her fingers over the engraved etching of Edward's name and the plaque below bearing Lorelai's name and credentials. 'I love these things. I've always wanted one but I've never been in one place long enough.' She touched Edward's plaque again, that deep need to truly belong filling her through and through. 'One day,' she murmured softly.

'Why is that?'

'Hmm?'

'Why have you never been in one place long enough?' And should he be worried about hiring a nomadic locum? Surely her wandering feet would stay grounded for the duration of her twelve-month contract. He'd make sure of it.

Honey shrugged. 'I guess I haven't found the place where I belong.' She turned to look at the scenery, sighing once more. 'It is extremely beautiful here.'

Edward watched her with interest, noting her effort to change the subject.

'It would be a fantastic place to raise a family. So peaceful with lots of open spaces and fresh air and…' She nodded. 'I could definitely raise my children here.'

'You have children?' Edward was stunned. What *had* Lorelai been thinking?

'Hmm? Uh…no. I meant in the future. Future children.' She waved a dismissive hand at him. 'Don't mind me. I'm just…' Another sigh. 'Dreaming.' She gazed at the scenery once more before turning back to him. 'You were raised here, weren't you?'

Surprised by the question, Edward found himself answering immediately. 'My parents moved here from Canberra when I was three, just before Mum had the twins.'

'Oh, it must have been wonderful.' She laughed, a sweet tinkling sound that seemed to blend in perfect harmony with the early-morning calls of the native birds. Edward felt a tightening in his gut at the sound and quickly turned away from her. With his gaze straight ahead, looking at the scenery that was usually quite calming to his senses, he couldn't believe what he saw. He blinked one slow blink as though to clear the picture before him but it didn't work.

'Your car's a little…bright, don't you think?' he asked, shielding his eyes against the glare shining off the paintwork from the early morning sunlight.

Honey smiled. 'It is. It has sentimental value but runs like a dream. Hubert gave it a complete tune before I left.'

'Hubert? Who's Hubert? Your…mechanic?'

She smiled. 'My grandfather. He likes to tinker with classic cars.' Honey looked lovingly at the small vehicle. 'It was a birthday present, which he enthusiastically restored for me.'

'So he chose the paint scheme?' Edward starting wondering whether Honey's entire family had rocks in their heads. He turned to look at her and found himself mesmerised by the smile touching her lips.

'No. I chose the colours and he knows my favourite flowers are daisies. He said I should try to stop fitting into this world because I was born to stand out.' Honey sighed and clutched her hands to her chest. As she stood there, the early-morning sun surrounding her, multicoloured hair loose and flowing over her shoulders, Edward sucked in a breath. There was a twinkle of happiness about her sparkling eyes, the tug of a smile evident on her perfectly sculpted mouth. Her face was completely devoid of make-up and he couldn't help but admit she was an extremely beautiful young woman.

'How old are you?' he blurted. 'You look about the same age as my youngest brother.'

'Oh? And how old is he?' she queried, seemingly not at all put out that he was questioning her in such a personal way.

'Er...he turned seventeen last month.'

'Ah. Right. Well, I'm *much* younger than him.' She pointed to the surgery behind where they stood. 'So... shall we go in? You can show me around and I can ask you three trillion questions so that by the time the patients start to arrive, I'm all hunky-dory with the set-up.' She raised her eyebrows. 'Yes?'

He didn't seem to be moving, still rooted to almost the same spot as when she'd first laid eyes on him. He was tall, about six feet four inches, she guessed. She liked tall men. 'Or I don't mind winging it if that's what you'd like. I'm very versatile and completely adaptable.' She raised her eyebrows in a teasing gesture and Edward was astonished to find his body reacting with increased heat and awareness.

'Adaptab—' Edward closed his eyes for a brief moment,

and pinched the bridge of his nose, needing to block the woman from his vision. He felt as though he'd just been sucked into some alternate dimension and that the last five minutes of his life had been one of total confusion and disbelief.

'Problem?' she queried.

He squared his shoulders and glared at her, trying not to be affected by her nearness or the hypnotic scent she brought with her. What was that perfume? It seemed to be a mixture of cinnamon and an earth-bound natural-ness with just a hint of something sweet and seductive. It was confusing his usually ordered mind. 'Yes, there's a problem. What do you mean, you're younger than my brother? Are you sure you're a qualified doctor?'

He'd obviously pigeonholed her. The clothes, the car, the colours in her hair, and he'd shoved her into a ste-reotypical box and labelled it 'fruitcake'. If that was the case, who was she to deny herself a bit of fun? 'Don't I *look* qualified?' Honey couldn't resist twirling slowly in a circle, swishing her hips, teasing him.

Edward swallowed the lump that instantly formed in his throat at her provocative movements. There was no doubt whatsoever that she was an incredibly attractive young woman and there was no doubt that she would cre-ate havoc amongst the single men in Oodnaminaby, in-cluding the elderly widowers. He instantly knew she was completely wrong for this town no matter how sensually appealing he might find her.

'In a word, no. You look as though you've just come from some bohemian fancy-dress fair, driving here in a car that looks as though you borrowed it from the circus.'

Honey pretended to frown. 'Shh. He'll hear you.'

Edward rolled his eyes. 'No wonder you and my brother get along. You both share that same warped sense of humour.' He dragged in a breath, trying to keep his calm so he could control this situation. 'What are you doing arriving so early in town? You weren't expected for at least another two hours. It's only just after six and every other town in the district is well over half a hour's drive away. Where did you start off from this morning?'

'Oh, I only came from Canberra. I stayed with friends last night and left just after four o'clock because I simply *adore* watching the sunrise. The way the colour starts to seep into the surroundings…' She stretched out her arms and wiggled her fingers, her movements adding a flourish to her words. She wore a few rings on her fingers, the jewellery sparkling in the morning light. 'Turning things from shades of grey to shades of green and blue and pink and orange, and it's just breath-taking.' She sighed and dropped her arms back to her sides. 'The show this morning certainly didn't disappoint.'

Edward blinked again, still unsure what to make of her. What on earth had Lorelai and Peter been thinking? This woman most certainly didn't fit the profile of a studious general practitioner. 'And your age?'

'Yes, yes. Of course. Sorry.' She smiled at him. 'In this stunning scenery, it's easy to get sidetracked. I'm seven and a quarter and quite proud of it. My birthday was only last week. Not a huge celebration like my last real birthday but still a spiffy one.'

'Seven and a…?' Edward's frown intensified but then it cleared. 'You were born on February twenty-ninth?'

Honey's answer was a wide and beaming smile. 'See. I knew there was a reason I liked you, Edward. You're quick. It usually takes people a good few minutes to figure it out.'

'You like me?' Her words stunned him a little. 'You don't even know me.'

'Ahh…that's where you're wrong. I've known Peter and Annabelle for years and I've met Peter's twin brother Bartholomew and both of them talk about you with such reverence and awe. Lorelai also thinks the world of you and it definitely takes a special man to do what you've done, Edward.' There was none of her earlier humour in her words and Edward realised she was completely serious with every word she spoke. It made him stop and take notice, intrigued by this different side of her.

'To be thrust into the role of father figure from the age of twenty-four,' Honey continued. 'To keep your family together, to put Bart and now Benedict through medical school, to keep your parents' dream of the family medical practice alive, and to do all of that while grieving for their loss…' Admiration lit her eyes and heartfelt emotion flowed through her words. 'That makes you quite a man, Edward Goldmark.'

'I had help,' he felt compelled to point out, lest she think he was a modern-day saint, which he wasn't. It was odd the way her words, her praise, the light in her violet eyes, shining with respect, made him feel as though he was someone important.

'I've no doubt about that. Lorelai told me how her father was always there for you, guiding you, offering advice, but when it came down to the bottom line, you made sacrifices for everyone around you, Edward, and that proves to me that you're a man of honour and great principle.'

Edward recrossed his arms over his chest, desperate to put up barriers between himself and this woman. He *had* made sacrifices for the sake of his family but he'd done it quietly, never once speaking out about the injustice he'd often felt. He'd put his brothers, the medical practice and the people of this community before himself and, while he didn't necessarily want any fuss to be made of his actions, it startled him that Honey was astute enough to see it.

'You're an old-fashioned gentleman whose word is his bond and I have to say it's not only a delight to find someone like you in this day and age but also that I am so honoured to be working alongside you for the next twelve months.' Honey's smile was bright, lighting her pretty features, and Edward felt mesmerised by her once more.

He'd just been about to tell her that he didn't think she was at all right for this practice. That even though Lorelai had made all the arrangements, he didn't think it was going to work out. That he appreciated her time but he could do without her help. It would be difficult, he would be burning the candle at both ends, but he'd survived worse. He could run the busy practice on his own for a few months until arrangements could be made for a more suitable locum.

Then she'd mentioned honour.

Honour *was* important to him and Lorelai had been acting on behalf of the practice, offering Honey a contract. Family *was* important to him and he wasn't sure he could bring himself to tell Peter that he thought Honey unsuitable for the position. Honesty *was* important to him and if he was completely honest with himself, he would accept that he *did* need Honey's help.

He realised there was obviously more to Honey than met the eye and that he'd be foolish to act impulsively. Besides, it wasn't his style. He was the type of man who thought everything through, who didn't make snap decisions.

'There are quite a few rules and regulations you'll be required to follow whilst working at the practice.' He spoke briskly.

'I wouldn't have expected anything less. Small communities are often very set in their ways and that's not always a bad thing.' Honey leaned forward and looked intently into Edward's brown eyes, a twinkle in her own. 'However, sometimes giving things a little bit of a shake-up is good for the soul. Right?'

Why did he get the distinct impression that she was talking directly about him and not the town? 'No.' He shook his index finger at her. '*No*. There will be *no* shaking-up...of *anything*.' Especially not him. He knew his brothers thought he was too set in his ways but Edward was a creature of habit. No beautiful, eccentric woman, barging her way into his world, was going to change that.

'This practice has run just fine since long before either of us was born. My parents built this practice up from the ground with the dream that it would be run as a family business, providing care and support to the people in these often isolated parts. The people who attend our clinic demand a certain level of care and I intend to see that standards are upheld so there will be no shaking up. Understood?'

'Absolutely. I agree with you one hundred per cent,' she said with a nod, her coloured hair shimmering in the morning sunlight as she inched towards him, allowing his preconceptions about her to work to her advantage. She'd seen the moment of hesitation in Edward's eyes as he'd looked at her and she'd had the feeling he'd been about to give her her marching orders. She couldn't let that happen. Oodnaminaby was calling to her, speaking to her in a way a place never had before. She needed to stay here, to discover whether this was the place she would finally find not only peace of mind but peace of heart.

'You won't know that peace until you feel it,' her grandfather had always said. 'But once you find it, oh,

Honeysuckle, darling, you hang onto it with all you've got.' She couldn't leave Oodnaminaby. Not yet.

'Well…uh…' Edward wanted to step back, to put some distance between himself and this woman who was slowly advancing towards him. 'Good.'

Honey took another step closer and whatever scent she was wearing teased at his senses. She angled her body inwards and said in a quiet, low but somehow sensual tone, 'It's nice to know we're on the same page, Edward, even if we're coming at it from different angles. Caring for people is a high priority on my list of lifetime goals. Good to know it's on yours, too.' Her gaze held his while she spoke, her words winding their way around him. Edward swallowed, his Adam's apple sliding up and down his throat. How was it she could make him feel so uncomfortable and so aware of her so easily?

When her gaze dipped to travel quickly over the length of his body, he couldn't help the tightening in his gut. She was attractive, she had sex appeal and it was clear she knew how to use it to disarm a man.

'I like a man of principle,' she said, her gaze meeting his again.

Edward couldn't contain his discomfort any more and, clearing his throat, he edged back, needing to put some distance between them. He uncrossed his arms, wanting to show her she didn't affect him at all. She was his locum for the next twelve months and, despite how wrong he might feel she was for the practice, he knew asking Honey to leave would bring questions not only from Peter but from Lorelai as well, and the last thing Lorelai needed in her heavily pregnant state was to think he'd doubted her judgement.

No, it appeared Honey was here to stay and he would have to do his level best to keep a safe distance between them. Their relationship would remain strictly professional. He took another step back and let his hands hang by his sides.

'Let me show you the clinic.' He was proud his words came out calm and controlled, brisk and professional.

'Edward…' she winked at him and took his hand in hers, tugging him towards the door of the clinic '…I thought you'd never ask.'

Momentarily stunned, allowing himself to be led into his own medical practice, Edward once again felt as though she'd knocked him off balance. It was an odd and dizzying sensation and for the first time since he'd learned of his parents' death he felt as though he really had no idea which way was up.

# CHAPTER TWO

'No, IT's perfectly all right,' Honey said as she escorted Mrs Etherington towards Reception. 'Of course you can take it with you. I make it up myself and it's never difficult to find empty jars.'

'And you're sure it will work wonders for my arthritis? Because I've tried everything else and nothing seems to give me relief.' Mrs Etherington held a small jar of white cream in her hands, hope in her eyes as she waited for Honey's reply.

'I'm sure it will but if after three days of applying the cream as I've shown you, you're not satisfied, come and see me. We could always try acupuncture.'

'Oh!' Mrs Etherington's eyes widened at this news but there was an excitement in her wise brown eyes.

'The most important thing is to find what's going to work for *you*.'

'Yes.' Mrs Etherington nodded. 'Thank you, Honey.'

'You are most welcome.' Honey smiled warmly. 'You have a lovely rest of the day.'

'Why, thank you, dear. Of course you need to be getting on with your patients. Don't let an old girl like me hold you up.' Smiling brightly, as she hadn't done in years, Mrs Etherington stopped to chat with some of her friends

who were in the waiting room, no doubt telling them all
about the new doctor.

Edward caught this exchange as he waited for Mr
Winton to manoeuvre his walking frame into the consulting room. In all the years he'd known Mrs Etherington,
he'd never seen her look so happy. He glanced at the waiting room, noting the curious delight on the faces of the
people. They were all looking at Honey as though she were
a new and exciting present they simply couldn't wait to
unwrap.

Honey, however, seemed oblivious to the wide-eyed
stares she was receiving and after spending a moment
with Ginny, saying something to make the sixty-three-
year-old receptionist smile, she picked up her next set of
case notes and called in her next patient. Mr de Mingo,
an elderly man who never seemed to move faster than a
snail, went eagerly with her, stepping sprightly.

Edward frowned, not happy she was handing out personal remedies to his patients. There could be anything
in that cream! What if things went wrong? *He* would be
the one to pick up the pieces, to pacify patients like Mrs
Etherington, who could be quite temperamental. No. This
wouldn't do at all. As soon as morning clinic was finished,
he'd have a quiet word with Honey and lay down the law.
He heard laughter coming from her consulting room, her
sweet tinkling sounds mixing with the deeper ones of Mr
de Mingo. Edward tried not to grit his teeth.

When Mr Winton cleared his throat and murmured
a husky 'Aren't you coming, Dr Goldmark?' Edward
snapped his thoughts back to the present, pushing his new
locum from his mind. He'd deal with her later.

As the morning progressed, Honey couldn't believe
how welcoming her patients were. There were one or two
who were naturally a little cautious, especially if she rec-

ommended an alternate course of treatment, but for the most part she thought things were moving along swimmingly.

From the moment she and Edward had entered the clinic that morning, Honey had been aware of the distance he maintained between them. She'd listened to his deep, modulated tones as he'd outlined the intricacies of the practice and what was expected of her.

He'd told her that in the summer months the town was often infiltrated with campers, hikers and fishermen, whilst in the winter months skiers, snowboarders and families wanting a winter break made up the visiting population. Although Lorelai had covered things in quite a bit of detail during their phone conversations, this was, to all intents and purposes, Edward's practice and as such Honey gave him her full attention.

She noted he was highly methodical, not wanting to leave anything to chance. He'd taken extra copies of her documents, saying they were for his own records, and she'd watched as he'd stapled everything together. Neat and tidy. Straight and organised.

Once the paperwork had been completed, he'd taken her on a tour of the clinic facilities, pointing out the location of the bathroom and kitchenette. He'd indicated where the receptionist—Ginny—sat, and the system for calling in patients.

'Ginny put the system in place and as she's been working here for as long as I can remember, we don't change it.'

'Warning me again not to rock the boat?' Honey had smiled brightly and Edward had shoved his hands into navy trousers as though her smile had been tempting him to touch her.

'Well…we wouldn't want to upset Ginny. Trying to get

her to use a computer a few years ago was bad enough,' he'd muttered, shaking his head. 'Still, she mastered it but wasn't happy for quite some time.'

'Contrary to what you might believe, I'm not here to upset anyone, Edward. I'm here to *help*.' Helping people was what she did. When she'd been a child, she'd helped animals, nursing them back to health with dedication and care. Her parents had been more than happy to encourage her to become a vet...until the day when she'd changed her mind, realising that human medicine was for her. They hadn't been so supportive then.

When Lorelai had arrived at about seven-thirty, the two women had embraced warmly, as though they were lifelong friends, excited to see each other again.

'You're far more beautiful in person than in photographs,' Lorelai said.

'You've seen pictures of me?' Honey had been surprised.

'Peter and Annabelle have some, from the time they visited you up in Queensland.'

'Oh, yes.' Honey had nodded. 'That was when I was in Port Douglas. My hair was shorter then and I think it was black.'

'Yes.' Lorelai had touched the multicoloured strands. 'But this style definitely suits you. You're so pretty.' Then Lorelai had turned and looked at Edward. 'Don't you think so?'

Put on the spot on a topic he'd rather not contemplate, Edward had quickly nodded and muttered something highly intellectual like 'Er...yes,' before excusing himself. He'd stayed in his clinic room until his first patient had arrived.

By the time lunchtime rolled around, Edward was eager to find out just how well his new colleague had coped with the clinic. He'd managed to find some time to peruse Honey's résumé and had to admit that she was almost over-qualified for a position as general practice locum. Aside from her medical qualifications, she held a degree in psychology and graduate diplomas in midwifery, naturopathy and acupuncture. It also stated that she was presently studying for her PhD.

It made him wonder, given she was only twenty-nine years of age, where she'd found the time to have a normal life. Part of him was streaked with jealousy that she'd been able to accomplish so much. He'd always intended to be a surgeon and, in fact, two days before his parents' deaths he'd been agonising over which university to apply to.

He'd had a rough plan for his life and had been in the midst of discussing his options with his parents when tragedy had struck. Not only had he then been responsible for his siblings but he'd had to give up the life he'd built for himself as a medical professional in Canberra.

And then there had been Amelia.

He breathed in deeply at the thought of the woman he'd been planning on marrying and still felt the slightest twinge of pain. It had been seven and a half years since he'd proposed to Amelia and seven and a half years since she'd rejected him. Even now he could hear her hurtful words.

'Edward. I love you. I really do but I'm not cut out to go and live in a little town and become an instant mother to grieving children. I've spent the past six years at medical school, I'm exhausted from my internship and marriage is so not on my agenda. And besides…' her eyes had lit with delight '…I was going to tell you later but I can't hide my excitement any longer. I've been accepted into the surgical training programme in Melbourne for next year. They don't usually accept interns so early but I made the cut. Isn't that fantastic?'

Edward closed his eyes and remembered how he'd murmured polite responses to her news. Amelia had continued to talk about herself for a while longer, brushing aside his proposal, and had had the audacity to ask him why he wasn't more excited for her.

Over the years he'd realised he'd had a lucky escape, not having been able to see before then how self-centred she was, but he knew he couldn't really blame Amelia. He'd been selfish in wanting her to give up her dreams, her goals, just for him. *He'd* had to make that sacrifice and he hadn't had a choice so it had been wrong of him to expect it of her... But if she'd really loved him, she would have been willing.

It wasn't that he didn't love his brothers, he did, even though Hamilton was driving him insane right now. Having his parents die just after he'd turned twenty-four, being legally responsible for his two younger brothers, had meant Edward had had to make certain sacrifices. Benedict had been only thirteen and Hamilton only nine. The twins, Peter and Bartholomew, had been twenty. Bart had been off attending medical school in Sydney and Peter had been getting ready to move out of home. Somehow they'd struggled through, managing to keep the family together, but all of his aspirations, dreams and hopes had died along with his parents.

Edward was pleased with what he'd managed to achieve, knowing it was what his parents had wanted. He'd held true to their legacy for their sons and he was grateful for the help he'd received both in and around the town of Oodnaminaby. But what of *his* dreams? Looking at Honey's résumé, seeing the scope of her experience and qualifications, he couldn't help but feel a little jealous.

No one had ever asked him what he'd really wanted in life. Everyone had always presumed he was quite content running the family practice and caring for his brothers, and in a way he was. He'd done what needed to be done but at the end of this year Hamilton would be finished at school and would probably move out.

Then what? He would have done his duty but what was he supposed to do next? He'd wanted to accomplish so much back then but now...things were different, *he* was different. What *did* he want to do next? His new locum seemed to have a direction for her life even if it was to find somewhere to one day raise her family. He could almost picture her with a gaggle of children around her, all of them with their arms out, twirling in the sunshine.

A slow smile touched his lips at the thought, then he shook his head to clear the image. He looked at Honey's résumé once more, noting her full name was Honeysuckle. Her surname was listed as Huntington-Smythe. Such a weird mix of a name.

He paused for a moment, then frowned, remembering he'd heard the name Huntington-Smythe before. It took only a second to recall, his eyes widening as his early-morning conversation with Honey replayed in his mind. 'Hubert Huntington-Smythe is her *grandfather*?' Before Professor Huntington-Smythe had retired, he had been one of Australia's leading pioneering neurosurgeons... and Honey was his granddaughter?

Edward put the document back into his in-tray and stood. Picking up his coffee cup, he headed out of his clinic room. When he walked into the kitchenette, he was surprised to find Lorelai sitting in a chair with her feet up on Honey's lap, his new colleague massaging Lorelai's feet. Neither woman seemed to notice his presence so he kept quiet, listening to Honey's smooth and modulated tones.

'Reflexology is more about pressure points. Acupuncture works on the same principle. Applying pressure to the base of your big toe helps to relieve abdominal and back pain, as well as releasing endorphins to help you relax.'

'Ooh, that feels so good,' Lorelai murmured, her head tilted back in the chair, her eyes closed. 'I feel so calm and the pain in my lower back has disappeared.' She sighed and sank down further into the chair.

'I can teach your husband exactly where he needs to be pressing so that during the birth he'll be able to help you.'

Lorelai opened her eyes slightly but didn't move. 'John won't do this. He hates it that I'm pregnant and refuses to be there for the birth.'

'Then *I'll* do this for you at the birth and if the pain gets bad at night, give me a call.' Honey's tone was still soothing and calm.

Edward clenched his jaw, unimpressed with Lorelai's husband. John wasn't his favourite person in the world but Lorelai had married him and therefore Edward and his brothers had done their best to get along with the man—for Lorelai's sake. They considered Lorelai and her father BJ as part of their extended family.

'What if I get a pain at three in the morning?' Lorelai asked.

'Then call me.' Honey's words were insistent. 'Enduring lower back pain when you don't have to will only lead to further discomfort. Besides, when I'm not working here at the clinic, I'm presuming I'll have quite a bit of free time. I'm not being polite, Lorelai. I'm quite serious.'

Lorelai sighed again and closed her eyes, her breathing once more nice and relaxed. 'I wish I'd known about these acupuncture pressure points before now,' she murmured.

Edward gritted his teeth, annoyed with another reference to acupuncture. 'If you melt into that chair any further, Lore, you're going to end up on the floor,' he murmured as he took his cup to the sink to rinse it.

'I don't care,' Lorelai replied, not bothering to open her eyes. 'Honey has managed to take away the pain I've been living with for the past few months.'

'You've been in pain?' Edward's tone was filled with instant concern.

'No more than any other pregnant woman who has only four weeks left to go.' Lorelai chuckled as she opened her eyes and smiled at her friend. 'Didn't I tell you I'd found the perfect doctor to replace me?' Lorelai looked from Edward back to Honey. 'Thank you, Honey.'

He watched as Honey continued to massage, kneading deeply. 'You're welcome. Helping people is why I became a doctor,' she replied, as a happy smile spread across her features.

Edward felt a tightening in his gut at the sight of those gorgeous lips of hers curving upwards and quickly turned back to the sink and washed out his cup. The more he looked at her, the more he couldn't believe how extraordinarily beautiful she was. There wasn't a scrap of make-up on her face, her multicoloured hair was tied back into a ponytail at the base of her neck with a red ribbon, and her Bohemian clothes were hardly what he would call stylish. In short, she was not the type of woman he was usually attracted to. In fact, she was quite the opposite and yet he was definitely attracted.

Edward glanced at the two women as he slowly dried his cup, watching Honey as she spoke in that calm tone of hers, relaxing Lorelai even further. Honey's neck was long and smooth and when he breathed in, that same scent he'd detected earlier that morning once more surrounded him. He became mesmerised by the way her arms and hands moved, the fluidity of her body, the way she seemed completely focused on her task, as though nothing else in the world mattered.

Exotic. Quixotic. Hypnotic.

'Lorelai?' Ginny walked into the kitchenette, bursting the bubble. Edward quickly turned and began filling the kettle, needing to do anything other than being caught staring at his new colleague. 'So this is where you all are.' The receptionist stopped and looked at the three of them. 'I'll have a tea, thanks, Edward,' Ginny said, after seeing him at the sink. 'Lorelai, your husband's on the phone...' There was a briskness to Ginny's words as though she really didn't like Lorelai's husband but her voice gentled as she continued. 'Honey, your first patient for the afternoon called to cancel so I've shifted some of Lorelai's patients onto your list.'

'Sounds great,' Honey replied, smiling at the receptionist before helping Lorelai out of the chair. 'In fact, give Edward and I all of Lorelai's patient's because she needs to be off her feet and at home, resting.'

'No. It's all right. I can...' Lorelai tried to protest but was cut off by a yawn. 'Oh. I think you've relaxed me too much.'

'Honey makes a valid point,' Edward interjected as he began making a cup of tea for Ginny. He turned and looked at the three women in the room. Two of them were like family—a surrogate mother and sister. The other one, well, she was just a new colleague. Nothing more. At least, that's what he seemed to need to tell himself over and over.

'And we don't want to argue with Edward,' Honey continued. 'Time to rest, Lorelai. Edward and I can hold down the fort.'

'Good idea,' Ginny agreed, as Lorelai tried again to protest but only succeeded in yawning once more. 'I'll see to it,' she said, ushering Lorelai out. 'You two need to get ready for afternoon clinic…but only after you've brought me a cup of tea,' she said with a twinkling smile.

Honey chuckled and the warm sound washed over him. He turned back to the task at hand, trying not to be conscious of the fact that they were both alone in the small kitchenette. He felt rather than saw her draw closer and hated himself for the heightened awareness he was feeling.

'I might have another cup of tea as well,' she said, coming to stand beside him. He shifted over, ensuring that not one part of his body touched hers. It didn't work, especially when she leaned across him to extract a cup from the cupboard, her bare upper arm brushing lightly across his chest.

She gasped at the touch, then turned to look up at him. 'Sorry.' Honey shook her head as though to clear her thoughts. 'I didn't mean to…nudge you.' Honey's mouth started to turn up at the corners. 'We *haven't* met before, have we, Edward?'

Edward swallowed, his Adam's apple sliding up and down his throat. His gut tightened as he realised she was watching his every action. If there was one thing he'd noticed so far today, it was that Honey gave her full attention to whoever she was with and right now all that attention was focused on him. He swallowed again. 'I think I'd remember.' Now why had his voice come out so deep, so husky, so mesmerised by the woman in front of him?

'So would I but I have the strangest sensation that we have definitely met.' She leaned in a little, her gaze dip-

ping momentarily to encompass his mouth. 'Maybe we
met in our dreams because there's a strange sort of…con-
nection between us, don't you think?'

'Uh…'

Honey paused a moment before shifting back and
reaching for his hand, holding his palm up in her own.
'You have nice hands. Hard-working hands. I think you
can tell a lot about a person simply from looking at their
hands.' She tenderly brushed her fingers across his palm,
somehow igniting every nerve ending in his entire body.
She swapped hands, caressing the other. 'Caring hands.'
She turned his hand over and caressed the back, her fingers stopping at a small scar at the base of his thumb.

Edward swallowed again and found he was powerless
to move, allowing the fresh scent she wore to once more
hypnotise him.

'How did you get this scar?'

'Uh…' He cleared his throat, willing his vocal cords—
and his mind—to work. 'I broke my thumb when I was
seven.' He gave a little shrug. 'Fell off my bike.'

Honey looked up into his eyes. 'Did you cry?'

'I tried not to.' He looked away from her penetrating
gaze, unable to believe how she could make him feel so…
special. It had been a very long time since *anyone* had
made him feel special.

'Brave. Even back then.' Honey bent and pressed her
lips to the scar and then released his hand.

'Wh-why did you do that?' he queried as he rubbed his
thumb, trying to dispel the wildfire of heat that was burning through him.

'What? Ask you questions or kiss your hand?'

'Both.'

Because I'm interested in getting to know you, not
only as a colleague but as a person. This is a small com-

munity where people tend to look beyond the occupation, the qualification or the title.'

'Ah...actually, speaking of titles,' he said, and edged back from her, desperate to put some much-needed distance between them. 'I noticed on your paperwork that your surname is Huntington-Smythe.'

'That's correct.'

'And that means your grandfather—Hubert Huntington-Smythe—was the world-renowned Australian neurosurgeon.'

'That's right. Until he retired a few years ago.'

'And started restoring cars?'

'Yes. He says the insides of the car are not that dissimilar to a human brain. His eyesight isn't what it used to be so he jokes that if he makes a mistake, it doesn't really matter. Jessica, my grandmother, is more than happy to have him home rather than working all hours at the hospital. The house was quiet when he wasn't there and I was always so worried we'd get a call and be told that he'd had a heart attack due to the stress but thankfully that didn't happen.'

'You lived with them?'

Honey nodded and finished making her tea. 'Since I was eighteen.'

This surprised him. From the way she dressed and her outlandishly coloured hair, she didn't appear to be the sort of woman who had been raised in a well-to-do household. She was such a contradiction he couldn't quite figure her out. He decided to try and dig a little deeper. 'And what about your parents? Did they live with them as well?'

'No. No, my mother ran away from home just after she turned seventeen, changed her name, married my father. They travelled from place to place, living the alternative lifestyle in communes and squats, always protesting against any injustice no matter how big or small. She hasn't been in contact with her parents since.'

Edward listened closely, again realising there was more depth to Honey than first met the eye. 'Is that what you did? Ran away from home?' Edward asked, thinking of Hamilton at the back of his mind. His brother had just turned seventeen and was wanting to leave school now, not bothering to finish his final year. He kept threatening to go live in Canberra with Bart, saying that he would leave home because Edward was a controlling tyrant.

Honey shook her head. 'I was eighteen. I *left* home as a legal adult. Big difference.'

'And went to live with your grandparents?'

'Yes. Jessica was lonely, especially with Hubert working so much. They put me through medical school and gave me the stability I'd always craved.'

'Stability? Your parents are unstable?'

She laughed without humour and shook her head. 'I guess it depends which way you look at it. They've been called hippies or gypsies or the more politically correct term of alternative lifestylers. By the time I turned eighteen, I'd realised that way of living wasn't for me, so I did something about it. I left.'

Edward continued to process what she was saying. 'Wait a second.' He held up his hand. 'If your mother is Hubert's daughter, how come your surname is Huntington-Smythe?'

'I changed it. In essence, I guess you could say I took on the life my mother rejected. She felt suffocated by the rules and regulations my grandparents had stipulated but I seemed to thrive in that environment. Children, even young adults, need boundaries.' Honey frowned for a moment.

'Your parents didn't give you boundaries?'

'Raised my brother and I free and natural, as they used to term it.' She shook her head. 'I left, I went to live with my grandparents and to honour them, I took their surname.'

'So…what *was* your surname?'

She shrugged one bare, elegant shoulder. 'Moon-Pie.'

He blinked one slow blink. 'Moon-Pie?'

'Go ahead. Make all the jokes you want. I've heard them all. My brother and I were teased at every different school we went to. Honeysuckle Lilly-Pilly Moon-Pie.'

'That's…quite a name.'

'Tell me about it. I'm going to call my daughter something easy, like Clara or Elizabeth. Something…normal that you can easily find on a door plaque for their bedroom door.'

'So now your name is Honeysuckle Lilly-Pilly Huntington-Smythe?'

'It is.' She angled her head to the side, her hair still secured by the shiny red ribbon, and Edward found himself momentarily distracted by her soft, smooth skin.

It had been one thing to ogle her neck from across the room but it was quite a different matter altogether to ogle it when she was right in front of him. He worked hard to control his breathing, to keep his desire under wraps. He cleared his throat and edged back a bit more, far too aware of her body so close to his.

'Did changing it make you happy?'

'In some ways, yes. In other ways…I'm still searching.'

He nodded as though he completely understood. 'Aren't we all. I've always had to be what everyone else needed me to be. A father, a brother, a breadwinner, a disciplinarian.' He wasn't quite sure why he was telling her this. No doubt Peter had told her the story but it wasn't something Edward often talked openly about, mainly because everyone in town already knew his past. 'Even now with Hamilton, when I'm not sure how to deal with his utter stubbornness, I still have to stand firm, to be the one in charge. Some days, I just want to give it all a big miss.'

He frowned, momentarily lost in his own thoughts, but when he looked at Honey he could see empathy in her eyes. He instantly straightened, wishing he hadn't revealed so much to a woman he barely knew. She was his locum. He was her boss. He couldn't allow himself to be drawn in by her natural charm, even though it felt like she had the ability to see right through his barriers. That was just another reason why he needed to keep her at arm's length.

'We're governed by the rules that bind us,' she stated with a knowing nod.

'And speaking of rules, I have something I need to say,' Edward continued, collecting his teacup and Ginny's, his tone becoming more sharp. 'I'd appreciate it if you didn't hand out your own personal remedies to the patients. If something were to go wrong, the malpractice insurance might not cover it.' He started to walk out of the room, pleased at the distance he'd managed to find, both literally and figuratively. Being so close to Honey, having her kiss his hand, had temporarily blinded him to his initial purpose, but now he was back and he needed to be sure she understood her position in this clinic.

'The use of acupuncture needles is also out of the question and I'd appreciate it if, starting from tomorrow, you would wear something more befitting a qualified general practitioner.'

With one firm nod Edward turned and walked from the kitchenette, no doubt leaving a bemused and bewildered Honeysuckle Huntington-Smythe in his wake.

# CHAPTER THREE

THE rest of the clinic proceeded without a hitch and by the time Ginny announced they were done for the day, Honey was starting to feel the fatiguing results of her early-morning start.

'Do you know where I'm supposed to be living for the next year?' Honey asked the receptionist as she handed up the last of the completed case notes.

'Oh, dear, Honey. I'm so sorry.' Ginny hunted around on her desk for a set of keys. 'Lorelai was going to take you over after clinic and show you around because Edward was supposed to have a house call in Adaminaby but that's been cancelled. She left the keys with me... Ah...here they are.' Ginny handed them over, then switched off her computer and picked up her bag.

'Where is—?'

'I'd take you there myself but I have to go and pick my husband up from Tumut and I'm already late. He's part of the amateur theatre group there and it does him good to get out of the house but as he doesn't drive any more after his stroke, it's up to me to get him there and back.'

'Well if you could just let me know where the—'

Ginny wasn't paying attention as she bustled around to the door. 'Sorry. Don't like dashing off on your first night here but I'm sure you'll be fine. Edward will look after you. Have a good night, Honey.'

Honey held out the bunch of keys Ginny had handed her. 'Well, if you tell me where the—' She stopped as the clinic door tinkled closed and Ginny disappeared. Honey sighed and looked down at the keys in her hand. She wasn't sure she wanted to ask Edward anything after the way he'd laid down the law. She knew he had every right to dictate the way she treated the patients but she felt he was out of line regarding the way she dressed. It wasn't as though she was filthy or indecent. She simply dressed differently. Still, it wasn't the first time she'd encountered such a close-minded attitude and she'd survived through worse. Tomorrow she'd dress the way he wanted because she really wanted to give Oodnaminaby a chance. First, though, she had to find out where she was staying and that meant asking her new fuddy-duddy colleague for his help.

'Problem?' Edward's deep voice came from behind her and she turned to see him leaning against the reception counter, a stack of case notes next to him. She was glad he couldn't read her thoughts.

Honey indicated the keys in her hand. 'Apparently I have a place to live in and I have the keys to the castle but unfortunately I have no idea where my palace is situated.' She shrugged. 'I guess Ginny was in a bit of a rush.'

Edward nodded. 'She has to pick up Harry from Tumut.'

'So she mentioned. I don't suppose you know where I'm living?'

'As a matter of fact, I do.' He jerked a thumb over his shoulder. 'Let me show you how we lock up and then I'll take you over.'

'Or you could just give me the address and once we've locked up, I'll get out of your hair.'

Edward shrugged. 'It won't take long.'

As Edward went through the lock-up procedures, she listened attentively, knowing there would be times when this would be a part of her duties. Once they were done, she collected her bag and car keys, heading out the front door. Edward put the alarm on and followed her, dead-bolting the surgery door.

'How's the rate of crime in Oodnaminaby?' she asked as she walked down to her car.

'Basically non-existent but with the equipment and drugs in the surgery—'

'Oh, I wasn't criticising,' she interjected. 'I was simply curious.'

'We have two full-time police officers but they cover a wide territory and work closely with the Kosciuszko National Park rangers.'

'Good to know.' She opened her car door and waited for Edward to give her directions. 'So…where am I headed? Left or right? Up or down?'

'It's not far.' He walked to the passenger seat. 'Better if I show you rather than tell you,' he remarked, feeling highly self-conscious as he climbed into the brightly co-loured, daisy-covered car. 'It really is…pink.'

Honey was about to protest, but his attitude was a lit-tle more relaxed than before and perhaps she'd been too quick to judge him. She smiled and nodded. 'I guess here it does seem a little over the top but I do love it and given I only really have a birthday every four years, the pres-ents become all the more special.'

'Fair enough.' He tried to ignore the way her fresh scent wound its way around him in the small confines of the ve-hicle. How was it that after travelling since four o'clock in the morning as well as doing a very full clinic, she could still smell so incredibly sweet? He cleared his throat, re-turning his thoughts to the task at hand. 'Er…turn left at the end of the car park, then up the hill and then turn into the third street on the right.'

Honey nodded, easily remembering his instructions. 'Where to after that?' she asked.

'Nowhere. You will have arrived at your destination. Oodnaminaby isn't that big.'

'So where exactly am I staying?' Honey turned into the third street on the right and slowed down.

'The coach house. Many years ago, it housed the horses and carriages of the early Australian pioneers but today it's been renovated with all the comforts of home. It's at the rear of my house.'

'*Your* house?'

'Problem?'

'Uh...no. None at all.' Honey wasn't sure how well she'd manage working and living so close to Edward. 'Actually, didn't Peter and Annabelle live in the coach house at some time? I thought I remembered her saying—'

'Yes, they did,' he confirmed. 'For the first year after they were married.' Edward nodded and pointed to the large family home built on stilts and with a sloping A-frame roof. 'It's this one here.'

'Wow.' She pulled the car into the driveway and came to a complete stop. 'Unbelievable!'

'What is?' He was a little confused.

'This place. It's just how I imagined it would be.'

'You imagined what my house looked like?'

'Not specifically your place. You know, the type of place that dreams are made of. It's a complete picture, what with the house, the trees, the garden, the scent of possibility in the air. Everything is beautiful and just... perfect.' She pointed to the different things as she un-clipped her seat belt and climbed from the car. 'Lovely, lovely, lovely.' She clapped her hands in delight, her face alive with happiness. 'I've never lived in a house with a sloping roof before. Excitement plus.'

'It's just a roof, Honey, and, besides, you'll be staying in the coach house, around the back,' Edward remarked as he unfolded himself from her small car, unable to stop watching the way Honey seemed to be drinking in the sights before her, eyes wide in wonderment. He stopped and looked at his property, trying to see it the way she did, but he shook his head. It was simply a house. Nothing more.

'It may be just a roof to you but to me it's a new and exciting experience. Everything in life can be seen as a new and exciting experience if you look at it the right way.'

'You're a real nature girl, aren't you,' he stated rhetorically, trying not to drink in every aspect of her inner beauty, which seemed to be shining out, illuminating her. She came and stood beside him.

'Do you get much snow here in winter?'

'Quite a bit.'

'Ooh. I can't wait.' Excitement burst forth as once again she was struck with the feeling that Oodnaminaby was special.

'You've never seen snow?' Edward raised his eyebrows at the question.

'Oh, sure I have. I've had holidays at the Australian snowfields over the years, I've skied in Switzerland, France and Austria. All beautiful, all fantastic, but I've never *lived* in a sub-alpine town before, hence the happy Honey you see before you.' Then with utter glee shining from her gorgeous face, she all but skipped up the driveway.

'Come on,' she called, beckoning to him. 'You have to show me *everything.*'

Edward knew she wasn't going to take no for an answer so went with her, quickly catching her up.

'Beautiful!' She waved her free hand at the colours, the floral scents from the row of flowers that lined the drive, the birds chirping in the air, the present blue sky with only a few fluffy clouds, the reds and oranges of sunset starting to filter their way through.

They came around the coach house and to her immense delight, opposite the door, Honey found the most incredible little garden with a rockery around the edge and stone steps leading down to a perfectly manicured patch of grass.

'Oh, my!' she breathed, stopping still so suddenly that Edward almost bumped into her.

'This is…' She stopped, as pleasure, awe and fascination at the beautiful garden engulfed her. It was clear that it had been lovingly cared for as there didn't seem to be any weeds anywhere. There were neatly trimmed hedges, tidy shrubs, native flowering plants and trees, and a bird-bath with a feeder in the centre. As they stood there, Honey drinking in the sights, two bright red and green rosellas flew down and started pecking at the seed and fluffing their feathers in the water.

'Don't move,' she whispered.

'Wouldn't dream of it,' he answered, and Honey was secretly delighted to find that Edward didn't think stopping and watching two birds was a silly thing to do. Kennedy had, but, then, Kennedy's idea of slowing down was to actually stop walking before drinking his coffee. Still, being in this stress-releasing garden was not the time to ponder her past relationship with Kennedy. They hadn't been able to agree on what they really wanted out of life, so Honey had ended it. That had been over five years ago and now she was standing looking out over one of the prettiest gar dens she'd ever seen, watching two little birds having fun in the water. A moment later they shook themselves then flew off, chirping to each other.

'The garden is...breath-taking, Edward.' As she kept looking, she noticed new and different things. 'Oh, look. There's a seat.' As she headed over, she realised it was engraved.

'FOR HANNAH AND CAMERON. YOUR LOVE ENDURES FOREVER.'

She turned to face Edward, her hands clutched to her heart, her eyes filled with a mixture of sadness and happiness. 'Aw...that's a lovely dedication.'

He nodded, astonished to find his throat thickening with emotion and in that one split second, with Honey by his side, looking down at the bench, the pain and loss of his parents' deaths settled over Edward again. He hadn't felt this way since he and his family had scattered their parents' ashes into the wind and he'd said goodbye.

'My...uh...' He stopped and cleared his throat. 'My mother planted this garden. So many years ago. It was *her* garden. Always has been, always will be.'

'Hannah's garden.' Honey spoke the name out loud and then nodded. 'It *does* suit it and you've kept it tended in her memory.' She looked up at him and Edward was surprised to see tears glistening in her eyes. 'That's perfect, Edward.'

'It's not meant to upset people.' He shifted away, feeling if he stood there for too much longer, looking down into her shining face, he'd end up giving in to the urge to hold her hand, to touch her, to pull her close and wrap his arms around her. It was an odd sensation to be so attracted to a woman he'd only just met. Still, deep down he appreciated that whilst this was *his* mother they were talking about, Honey was the one overcome with emotion.

Honey sniffed and laughed. 'Sorry. I'm a highly emotional being, especially when I discover something extraordinary. Peter's shown me pictures of your mother and I can quite easily imagine her here, wide straw hat on her head, kneeling on a rug as she pulls weeds or trims the bushes.'

'Yes.' Edward exhaled slowly, a sense of calm settling over him. 'You know it's odd, I come out here and look after the garden, so does Peter and BJ, Lorelai's father, and even Hamilton mows the grass and pulls the odd weed or two. Sometimes Lorelai comes, more often than not lately, and we all do our little bit to keep it neat and tidy, but I think this is the first time in a long while that I've just stood and appreciated it.' He put his hands on his hips and nodded, slowly turning as though drinking in what the combined efforts of his family had produced. 'My mother planted this.' He spoke the words as though they were really only now penetrating his mind and Honey could hear that his voice was thick with emotion.

'She left you all a sanctuary and one that was designed and made from her heart, a heart filled with love. She must have been quite a mother, so loving, so caring, so thoughtful.'

'Yes.' He looked at Honey for another moment then turned his back but not before Honey had seen his eyes become glazed with repressed sorrow. She wondered how much he'd actually been able to grieve for his parents before the heavy burden of responsibility had settled on his broad shoulders.

Honey moved further into the centre of the garden and looked around her, wanting to give Edward some space. She sniffed a flower or two, watched the bees and admired the view of the rolling hills beyond, the colours of the sky beginning to intensify even more. Her heart filled with pleasure as the small daffodils danced nearby.

'It's so incredibly perfect,' she whispered, then, unable to contain her joy any longer, she put her arms out and her head back and twirled around. Edward watched, captivated by the freeness of her heart. Honey seemed to see the world he thought mundane and restricting as wild and free. The first time he'd seen her twirl like this, he'd thought she was quietly insane, but now it seemed right that she would appreciate such beauty in such a way.

'Don't you think it's lovely?' she said, but the instant the words were out of her mouth, she overbalanced and came tumbling down onto the grass.

'Honey!' With two long strides he was at her side, only to find her giggling with glee. He looked away, to the view beyond the garden, the sunset meeting the tops of the mountains. It was a view he'd seen for most of his life and of course he knew it was pretty, but actually stopping to look at the garden, at the view and really appreciating them was something he rarely did. However, the view was far safer than the enchanting woman at his feet.

Honey sat up, the smile still on her face. 'Why don't you sit down? Join me on my magic green carpet.' She stroked the grass. 'We can go *anywhere*!' She beckoned him down and he had the feeling that she wasn't going to let up so did as she asked.

'You're acting like a child,' he said, but there was no censure in his tone. It was more of a statement and one that held just the slightest hint of jealousy.

'Well, I am only seven and a quarter,' she pointed out matter-of-factly.

'A ready-made excuse. Lucky you.'

'You don't need an excuse to let go, Eddie. Everyone's entitled to reactivate the child within and just have a tantrum. Lie on the grass and kick your arms and legs, scream, yell, let it all out. Let your frustrations, your anger, your pain be expelled from your body. Come on. Try it.' She nodded enthusiastically. 'You'll feel great afterwards.'

'I am not going to lie down and yell.' His words were calm and well modulated and he shook his head for emphasis. Honey could see she was losing the battle...for now, but right then and there she accepted the mission to loosen Edward up and to help him deal with the repressed grief she could see behind his eyes. 'Is that what you used to do as a child? Lie down yelling, kicking and screaming out your frustrations?'

Edward had merely meant the question as a form of deflection and was astonished when he saw a slight flicker in the smile on her lips. An apology was already forming in his mind when she gave a tiny shrug and shook her head.

'No. There was never anyone around to pay attention. If you're going to have a full-on tantrum, you want witnesses. Anyway...' she patted the grass again '...why don't you tell me about your childhood? I love that you've lived in the one place for most of your life. How grounding that must have been.' Honey's eyes twinkled with anticipatory excitement and Edward had to admit she looked very becoming. 'What are some of the best memories you can think of about this garden and this house?'

'Why? So you can assess my psyche? I know you hold a degree in psychology. I'm not some broken toy you need to fix while you're working here.'

'I never said you were. Besides, if you stop to think about it, we're all broken in one way or another. We've all had our share of hurts and disappointments and they scurry around in our minds, finding places to hide like a Jack-in-the-box and then they *jump* out at us and go *blah*, unleashing those carefully boxed-up emotions all over the place. It's usually when we least expect it.'

'Really? So *you* have some...' He stopped, unable to say the words she'd used because they sounded silly.

'Jack-in-the boxes...' she encouraged.

'Hiding in your mind?' He finished.

'Of course.'

'What are they?'

Honey smiled as she ran her hand over the grass, liking the way it tickled her palm. 'Oh, where to start. Shall I lie down?'

Edward couldn't help the smile that spread across his lips. 'Sitting is fine, Dr Huntington-Smythe,' he remarked in his best doctor voice. Honey closed her eyes, took a deep cleansing breath and then slowly released it.

'I'm ready.' She opened her eyes. 'Ask what you will.'

'Just like that? You'll open up to me?'

'I'm hardly an espionage agent, Edward,' she responded with a smile.

'Uh...OK.' He thought of a question that was really burning in his mind. 'What brings the granddaughter of a classic, iconic surgeon all the way to Oodnaminaby for twelve months?'

'The opportunity to help people,' was her reply.

Edward watched her carefully. 'There's more to it than that,' he murmured.

'Possibly.'

Edward waited, keeping silent, knowing it would prompt her to expand on her answer.

Honey raised her eyebrows. 'You're really getting into the part of the psychologist,' she said after they'd sat in silence for a minute. 'All right, if you really want to know, I'm looking for a place where I can...truly belong.'

'And you think that might be Oodnaminaby?' His eyebrows were raised. Was she looking for a permanent job? Wanting to *live* here in town? A thousand different scenarios flooded through Edward's mind at the thought of this gorgeous woman living here, seeing her every day, around the town, infecting his clinic with her alternate remedies. Or worse…what if she started up her own medical practice, where if people weren't satisfied with the response at his clinic, they'd go to hers? What would that mean for his parents' legacy?

'I don't know.' Her words were honest.

Edward let out a deep breath, unaware he'd been holding it while waiting for her answer.

'I feel as though I've been looking far too long. Probably since I was about six years old.'

'Six years old? Or are you referring to when you were *really* one and a half?' He smiled and was pleased when she reciprocated.

'Yes. Only one and a half when I first remember my parents leaving me.'

His eyebrows raised. 'They left you?' Edward shook his head. 'I don't understand.'

'They went off to protest something or other, they were—still are—always protesting something. The bigger, the better as far as they're concerned. Clean water. Fresh air. Greenhouse emissions. Don't dam the river. Bring home the troops. Anything and everything. My brother calls them professional protesters and in a way he's right.'

'So…they went off to protest something and left you alone?' he prompted, eager to hear her story.

'Hardly alone. I was six years old and they left me "in charge" of my three-year-old brother, four-year-old twins and a ten-month-old baby. The baby and the twins belonged to two other families we were living with. Three sets of parents left the commune and didn't come home until three days later. In their defence, they thought they'd only be gone for a matter of hours but the peaceful protest turned not so peaceful and they were all arrested, spending two nights in gaol.'

Edward was stunned. 'And no one came to find you? Social services? Anyone?'

Honey shook her head. 'Nope. If they told social services about their children, they risked having us taken from them. When they returned, they were astonished I'd coped. I knew how to change nappies and I fed us all mashed potatoes because that's all I knew how to cook. Everyone went to bed on time and washed in the morning before they dressed. I was a right little mother.'

Honey folded her knees beneath her skirt then hugged them to her chest. 'As I coped so well at such a young age, they would often leave me in charge of several children. Animal healing and childminding. Those were my primary duties wherever we lived for the next decade.'

'And I'm sure you learned to cook more than mashed potato.'

Honey smiled, pleased he hadn't offered any empty platitudes. 'Yes, I did and my brother was forever grateful.'

'What do you mean by animal healing? Do you have magical powers?'

'Don't I wish.' She smiled. 'I would have magicked myself and Woody out of that life a lot earlier. No, the animal healing is what my father called it. When I was about five, I found an injured ring-tailed possum and I nursed it back to health. Splinted its little tail, fed it milk through an eyedropper, kept it warm, that sort of thing. After that, if anyone found an injured animal, it was brought my way.'

Edward shook his head, completely bemused. 'It sounds like a life that was never dull.'

'It sounds like a life that was never happy,' she counteracted, her voice barely above a whisper.

'You're looking for happiness, then?'

'Isn't everyone? I *did* find a level of happiness, though. When I left and went to live with my grandparents, I had people who cared about me, who were interested in *me*, not simply in what I could do for them. I was happy but I can't live with my grandparents for ever, now, can I,' she stated with a small smile.

'According to your résumé, you've certainly travelled a lot, working in different places for six- or twelve-month contracts.'

'The place that fits me has been rather elusive,' she agreed with a small nod. 'But I am determined to find my home. I can't give up because I simply know it's out there somewhere.'

'You don't see your parents at all?'

Honey looked away from him, into the stunning sunset that surrounded them. 'My parents and I have never seen eye to eye. You think I'm bad, offering patients an alternative to traditional medicine, but my parents are way off the charts as far as that goes.' Honey tried not to scowl as she remembered the way her mother had refused to have her pregnancy checked, even though she'd been in her mid-forties. The result had been disastrous. 'If there isn't a natural cure, they don't want to know. I'm not that closed minded, Edward. I was raised to use honey on bee-stings, to place aloe vera on rashes, to chew root ginger to relieve intense pain. It's true that we can learn a lot from nature but I also agree to prescribing antibiotics when warranted, that terminally ill patients should make use of the synthetic barbiturates as pain relief and that X-rays and ultrasounds are the inventions of complete geniuses.'

Honey put one hand over her eyes, willing her breathing to settle, willing for the peace she'd spent years learning to find to wash over her. With one deep breath she removed her hand and gave Edward a lopsided smile. 'Next question?'

Edward returned her smile, seeing that she was mentally exhausted. It was then he remembered she'd had a very long day. They were both silent for a moment, watching the changing colours of the sky. 'Do you think we'll see a star soon?'

Honey glanced at him, grateful he hadn't asked her another probing question. 'I hope so. I'd like to make a wish.'

'Wishing to find your home?'

Honey hugged her knees closer, her head back as she looked at the sky once more. 'Wishing for a happier future. For my children to have a life of stability and understanding. You had that. You had parents who loved you, who provided for you, who left you their legacy.' She ran her hand over the grass once more. 'Such a beautiful garden.'

'Thank you,' Edward said a minute or two later. 'I appreciate your openness, Honey. It's something I…struggle with…opening up to people,' he clarified.

'Well, you live in a town where everyone knows your story so it's not as though you'd have to repeat it all that often.'

'True.'

'But they don't know the *real* you, the man deep inside, do they?'

Edward slowly shook his head, still looking into her eyes. 'Sometimes I'm not even sure if *I* know me.'

'You've been wearing too many hats.'

He nodded, amazed at how well she seemed to under-stand him. 'Exactly.'

They both sat there on the grass, neither of them mov-ing, their gazes locked. He was captivated, watching her as they'd watched the rosellas, not daring to move a muscle as he appreciated the incredible beauty that was Honey. His heart started to pound beneath his chest and his palms began to sweat as he realised he was powerless to look away from her gorgeous eyes.

'What colour are your eyes?' he murmured softly. 'Sometimes they look blue, other times they're more like a violet colour.'

'They're bluey-greeny-grey but I'm wearing coloured contacts.' Her tone was as soft, and as intimate as his own. 'They sometimes appear to alter the colour of my irises. I have green contacts, too.'

It was odd. Sitting there. So close. Looking at her. Giving in to the urges he'd been fighting ever since they'd met. It was as though they were having two very different conversations. One was quiet and restrained, the other—the non-verbal one—was a rage of riotous emotions.

How was any man to ignore such a woman?

'Why do you colour your hair?' His hands were itching to reach out and touch it, to feel if it really was as silky as it looked.

Honey smiled and then without another word she re-moved the red ribbon and let her hair fall loosely around her shoulders, enticing him further. Then she reached up, fiddling with a clip or something at the top of her scalp. A second later he heard a faint 'click' and she removed an artificial plaited blue braid, holding it out to him.

'It's fake?'

'Well…that one is. So is the green one, but the others are real.'

'But why?' Unable to contain the need, he reached out and scooped a handful of her long hair from her shoulder, allowing it to sift through his fingers. It was as soft and as silky as it looked and it left his hand tingling with delight.

Honey tried not to gasp at his brief touch, swallowing lightly over the instant dryness of her throat. 'Why not?' she countered, not at all surprised that her words came out more huskily than she'd thought. 'It's just colour. Don't you think it suits me?'

Edward couldn't help but nod, even though he knew she was fishing. 'You know it does. You know you're beautiful, Honey, and that makes you dangerous to be around.'

She itched to lean forward, to close the distance between them, to throw her arms about his neck, to urge his head down so their lips could make contact, but she'd already sensed Edward was an old-fashioned type of man. She could nudge him a little but if she went too far, too soon, she'd scare him off for good and that was the last thing she wanted.

Slow and steady. She stayed where she was but angled her head slightly, her hair sliding off her shoulder to reveal her neck. She watched as Edward's gaze dipped momentarily to the smooth skin, his pupils dilating for a fraction of a second, indicating he liked what he saw. It made her feel all warm and fuzzy inside.

'Dangerous for whom?'

'For both of us. We don't fit, Honey. We come from two very different worlds and our lives appear to be heading in two very different directions.' He shook his head again before getting to his feet, brushing the grass from his navy trousers. 'Hamilton will be home from sport practice now so I'd better get inside and start dinner.' He took a few steps away from her, then turned. 'Welcome to Ood.'

## CHAPTER FOUR

THE next morning, Honey woke up feeling highly optimistic about the day ahead. She'd slept incredibly well and with the sunlight streaming in through the open curtains of the coach house she couldn't resist getting up and facing the dawn.

Looking out the kitchen window at Hannah's garden, she smiled as she pictured Hannah Goldmark working hard to make her garden sanctuary. As a mother with five boys, no doubt she would have needed it. Honey's thoughts turned to Edward and his impeccable manners…although she wasn't quite sure what he'd meant when he'd said they were a wrong fit.

There was no fooling herself about her attraction to him but that didn't necessarily mean she was ready to jump into a relationship. First, she wanted to get to know the town and the people, to see if Oodnaminaby really did possess the magic she was looking for, but she had to admit that Edward's comments had piqued her interest. If she was going to do a psychological evaluation on her new colleague, she'd say he'd been caught so tightly in a web of duty he wasn't sure how to get out. Had he denied himself any sort of private life during the past eight years since his parents' deaths? Had he ever really had the time to come to terms with their loss before he'd stepped up to the plate and taken over the reins?

'You raised a good, strong man, Hannah.' She aimed her words towards the garden. Even yesterday evening, after he'd turned and walked away, she'd found him later, with his youngest brother, out at her car, unloading her belongings.

'G'day,' Hamilton had said when he'd spotted her. 'Nice wheels.'

'Thanks,' Honey remarked, after introducing herself.

'Do you think I'd be able to score a drive some time?'

'Hamilton,' Edward warned, but Honey laughed and held up her hands to show she hadn't taken offence at Hamilton's enthusiasm.

'It takes a secure man to drive around in a hot-pink, daisy-covered car,' she pointed out, but nodded. 'If you'd like to go for a drive, we can.'

'Now?' Hamilton pushed.

'Homework,' Edward growled as he lifted two canvas bags from the back seat and thrust them both at his brother. 'Take these to the coach house.'

'I'm sitting my driver's licence test next week,' Hamilton continued brightly as he headed up the driveway.

'Heaven help us,' Edward murmured, and Honey couldn't help but smile.

'He's not that wild, is he?' she asked as she opened the boot to reveal two boxes.

'Pete's been teaching him to drive because I simply wouldn't have the patience.' Edward pointed to the boxes. 'Is this it?'

'Yep.'

'You travel light.'

'For a woman,' she added.

'I didn't say that,' he countered, taking out one of the boxes.

'Ah, but you were thinking it.' Honey had removed the other one, shut the boot, then headed up the driveway.

Within another five minutes she'd been officially installed at the coach house. Edward had outlined the facilities, with Hamilton shifting back and forth around the place, pointing out different white goods as Edward rattled them off. 'You have a fully equipped kitchen, washer and drier, bathroom and sitting room downstairs with the bedroom upstairs.'

Hamilton's teenage comedic antics had made Honey laugh as he'd ended up pointing upstairs as though he were directing an aeroplane, both hands pointed forward towards the stairs. Edward had rolled his eyes but Honey was positive she'd seen his mouth twitch.

'You'll also find bread, milk, sugar, tea and coffee in the cupboards and fridge.'

Hamilton had skidded around the floor, opening the cupboards and then the fridge, swiping his hand through the air as though he'd been a model on a game show. Honey hadn't been able to resist laughing again.

'Clown,' Edward had murmured, which had only made Honey giggle even more. 'Go have a shower before you slide and crash into something,' he'd instructed his brother, his tone not as brisk as it had been before. Hamilton bowed, a wide grin on his face, before waving to Honey as he'd left the coach house, leaving Honey and Edward alone again.

'Thank you, Edward,' Honey murmured, stepping over one of the boxes she'd carried in, coming closer to his side. 'The coach house is perfect.' She looked around the room, admiring the décor. 'You've been more than helpful—with everything.' Before he could leave, she quickly leaned up and pressed a kiss to his cheek.

'What was that for?'

She shrugged. 'For making me feel welcome.'

Edward had held her gaze for a moment longer before he nodded once, then turned and headed out the door.

Honey sighed and closed her eyes, wishing she'd been able to read his mind. The kiss to his cheek had been prompted by an overwhelming sense of thankfulness. In some of the towns she'd worked at over the past five years since her break-up with Kennedy, she'd either spent the entire time in a rented room in a rundown hotel or in an apartment with the barest furnishings. Compared to most of the places, the coach house was pure luxury and Edward's thoughtfulness in providing her with the basics had been the cherry on top.

She hadn't expected him to understand how she'd felt but even though he'd asked her to tone down her outfits and to refrain from giving patients alternate treatments, he'd still taken the time to ensure she was settled.

'Yes, Hannah, you raised a good man,' she said again, and looking out at the perfect morning spread before her. Unable to contain the happiness that bubbled through her, Honey flung open the door and skipped out into the garden, breathing in the freshness of the day, and lifted her voice in song.

When he first opened his eyes, Edward could have sworn he heard singing. He checked the clock. It was just after six and for a moment he thought he'd set his radio alarm to the wrong station. No. His alarm wasn't supposed to click in for another half an hour. So where was that singing coming from?

No doubt Hamilton had turned on a radio somewhere

but after a moment of lying in his bed and listening to the sounds of the house he realised it wasn't a radio. He rubbed his eyes as he climbed from the bed and stretched. Pulling on a pair of jeans, he padded barefoot down to the kitchen and turned on the coffee machine. While he was waiting, he headed to the window and opened the blind, squinting as he peered out into the morning sunshine. The house was quiet, the world outside was still, but he could definitely hear the faint strains of a beautiful voice.

He gazed towards the coach house and then nodded, realisation dawning on him. *That* was where the singing was coming from. Honeysuckle. One of the most mind-blowing, off-the-wall, disruptive women he'd ever encountered. It was now twenty-four hours since they'd met and yet he felt as though he'd known her for much longer.

Grabbing a cup of coffee, he opened the back door and stepped out, breathing in the brisk air before sipping his hot drink, which warmed him through. He probably should have stopped to pull on a T-shirt and some shoes but he was intrigued. The singing was louder outside and he realised that Honey wasn't in the coach house, as he'd originally thought, but somewhere in the garden.

Walking gingerly in his bare feet on the cold ground, Edward went in search of the early morning songbird and around to the side of the coach house. He found her—in the small garden his mother had loved. Honey was standing barefoot in the grass. She had flowers, shrubs and trees around her and her arms were out to the sides, her eyes closed, her face tipped towards the sky. His gaze travelled over her, taking in the singlet top and the love-heart cotton pyjama bottoms she wore, her long, multicoloured hair scrunched messily into a hair band, tendrils escaping here and there as though refusing to be bound.

As the last note of her song died upon her lips, she

breathed in deeply then sighed. Birds in the nearby tree seemed to chirp in appreciation, almost as though they were cheering her. A smile spread across her lips and Edward was suddenly pierced with an overwhelming sense of jealousy and longing. To be so free, so happy, as Honey looked right now... He shook his head, clearing the emotion as quickly as it had come.

'That was beautiful,' he remarked, knowing he should announce his presence sooner rather than later, lest she turn and think he was spying on her. Her feet remained stable as she looked at him over her shoulder.

'Oh. I'm sorry if I woke you. I didn't...mean...' Her words faltered as she took in his state of undress. Swallowing over the sudden dryness in her throat, Honey couldn't help the way her gaze lingered on his lightly tanned bare chest. He wasn't hairy like her father or even pale skinned like her brother and whilst she was a trained medical professional and had seen many a naked chest before, this was entirely different. This was *Edward*, the man she hadn't been able to stop thinking about.

Her heart did a little flip-flop as her tongue slipped out to moisten her lips. Her eyelids fluttered closed for a split second as she tried to reboot her brain so she didn't end up a babbling twit in front of such a handsome man.

'It...er...was such a beautiful morning and the song just burst out.' She gave a slight shrug of her shoulders.

Edward sipped his coffee, his male pride secretly pleased with the way she'd given him more than just a cursory glance. His skin was not only being warmed by the rising sun but also by her appreciative gaze.

When he didn't say anything else, Honey turned her attention back to the flora nearby and bent to breathe in the scent of the beautiful flowers. Anything to stop herself from ogling Edward again, even though she desperately wanted to sneak another long look. She walked to the stone bench and brushed her fingers across the engraved words. 'Do you miss them?'

'Every day.'

She turned to look at him then, glad he hadn't moved and that there was still a good distance between them. 'I can't imagine what it must have been like for you, to lose both of them at the same time. No wonder you're searching for some peace.'

'Who said I'm searching for peace? Was it Peter? Or Lorelai?'

Honey raised her eyebrows. 'It was neither of them.'

'Then what makes you say I want peace?'

'Uh…how about the way you're flipping out right now?' She smiled at him, as though she was indulging him.

'I am not flipping…' He stopped and raked his free hand through his hair.

'You haven't had time to grieve properly for your parents.' Honey's voice gentled. 'You had a lot on your mind back then, and have had for the last eight years. Have you at least had a holiday? Gone away for a good long break?'

'Of course,' he said. 'I used to take Ben and Hamilton away for a few nights every holidays. Sometimes we'd go canoeing or hiking. In winter, we'd go skiing or snowboarding. Lots of camping, lots of outdoorsy stuff.'

'Great. It's good for stress release.'

'Exactly.'

'But did you ever go away…on your own…just you?'

'I don't have time for those types of vacations, Honey. Between the clinic and home and conferences and eating and sleeping and—'

She held up her hands and he stopped. 'I get the picture.' She paused for a moment and Edward had the strangest sensation she was trying to choose her words carefully. 'Would you consider going away now? Just you? By yourself for...' she shrugged '...a few nights?'

'I can't. Lorelai's just taken maternity leave and, besides, Hamilton needs stability, someone to stand over him so he gets his homework done.' There it was again, just a slight hint that something was going on between the two brothers. Honey filed the knowledge away for now. It was clear Edward was stalling, putting obstacles in his own way to avoid the pain and hurt that had been buried deep within him for the past eight years. She also realised there was no point in pushing him, not just yet.

He sipped his coffee and stuck his other hand into the pocket of his old denim jeans. Seeing him standing there, Honey couldn't help but contrast this picture with the man she'd met yesterday morning at a similar time. The man yesterday had been dressed, defensive and determined. This man was raw, impatient and demanding. Honey also realised she was equally attracted to both aspects of the man but, then, what female wouldn't be? Edward Goldmark was definitely quite a catch and while she hadn't come to town looking for a relationship, she was starting to realise she couldn't completely rule it out.

'Life has a funny way of sneaking up on you,' her grandfather had often said. 'One day, Honeysuckle, you're going to find the man that fits perfectly with you. Your heart nestled comfortably with his. That's the way it was with me and your grandmother and although we've had our ups and downs over the years, we've never let go of each other's heart.' Hubert had nodded. 'It'll happen. One day. Just you wait. You won't be expecting it, girl, but it'll happen.'

Honey tried not to stare at Edward's firm, sculpted chest but it was difficult when the man was so incredibly gorgeous. 'What about—?' she began, but stopped then closed her eyes, trying to catch the train of thought she'd just lost.

'What about...what?' he asked a moment later.

'Uh...' Honey opened her eyes, forcing herself to look directly into his. 'I've, uh...forgotten what I was, uh... Hey, would you mind putting on a T-shirt or a jumper or something? Please?'

'Oh?' Edward looked down at his naked torso, an unbidden slow smile spreading across his lips as he realised why Honey had been a little jumpy. 'Sorry. I guess I'm not used to having a woman around the place.'

'Fair enough, but this is your one warning. Dress all bare and sexy like that again and I don't know if I'll be able to control myself.' She winked at him, adding punch to her words.

He blinked twice, utterly shocked at the way her open and honest words burned through him, igniting the flame of deep, primal need. He'd never felt anything so intense or powerful before. 'Uh...yeah.' He eventually nodded. 'Point taken.' He turned and took a few steps away before she called his name.

'I remembered what I was going to say.'

'What's that?' he asked, mildly embarrassed when his words came out a little huskily. It wasn't every day that a beautiful woman told him she found him sexy. Clearly, she'd affected him.

'Are you free on Saturday?'

'Saturday?' he frowned. 'Why?'

'So you can meet me after morning clinic.'

'And why would I do that?' He took a sip of his coffee, needing to do something other than stare at her in those tight little pyjamas she was wearing, which did absolutely nothing to hide the luscious curves of her body. 'What do you want to do?'

Honey's smile slowly widened, her eyes twinkling with delight. 'What will we do?' She asked, her tone deep and sultry and sexy, and he wasn't at all sure whether or not she was teasing but right now all he could do was swallow and watch as she came to stand before him. 'That's for me to know and for you to find out, mister.'

When Edward turned up at the clinic later that morning, dressed appropriately in his usual trousers and polo shirt, his tongue nearly rolled out of his mouth and hit the floor when he saw a sleek, professionally dressed Honey in the kitchenette, making herself a cup of herbal tea.

'Hi, again.' She smiled and held up an empty mug. 'Tea?'

'Uh…ah…' Edward stopped trying to speak and simply blinked a few times to clear his vision. Honey was dressed in a grey pinstriped pencil skirt, which came to just above her knees, her legs were bare and her feet were enclosed in a pair of sensible court shoes. She wore a matching jacket and a cream blouse. Her hair was pulled up into a chignon and he could only see one or two glimpses of the different coloured strands blending with her honey-blonde locks. She wore a touch of mascara and lip gloss, her jewellery kept to a minimum.

In essence, she was the consummate medical professional, the general practitioner he had initially expected to appear on his doorstep yesterday morning—Dr Honey Huntington-Smythe. Yesterday he'd found her attractive, even though she wasn't his type. Today made him realise that it honestly didn't matter what she was wearing—loose swirly skirts and tops, tight-fitting pyjamas or a pinstripe suit—the woman was absolutely stunning and he was having the most difficult time *thinking* around her.

That had never happened before. Not with any of his other colleagues, not with any of the girls he'd dated during medical school and his internship, and it most certainly hadn't happened with Amelia. He'd always managed to appreciate their looks, to acknowledge their beauty and to keep his brain functioning with no ill effects whatsoever, yet Honey turned him into a blithering idiot with one simple smile.

'I'll take that as a yes,' she replied and placed a teabag into the empty mug. 'Did Hamilton catch the school bus all right this morning?'

'What? Huh?'

Her smile increased. She hadn't expected her clothes to have such a paralysing effect on Edward but she was extremely pleased they had. She'd learned years ago that in order to fit in more smoothly with people, she needed to dress a certain way. Power dressing was what her grandmother had called it and together they'd gone shopping for just the right outfits.

'Remember, Honeysuckle,' Jessica had said. 'They're just clothes. Clothes do not make the woman—the woman makes the clothes. It doesn't matter whether you're wearing three-piece suits or lacy-frilly things, you be yourself. Always.'

And she had. During her internship, she'd wear her suits to work, blending in like everyone else, but as soon as she arrived home she'd change into her 'hippy', freer-flowing clothes, feeling as though her soul could breathe once more. Today, though, it had been well worth the effort to see Edward's reaction. Besides, she was only doing what he'd asked.

For the rest of the week Honey wore the suits, with

Ginny remarking that she looked very fancy, very swish, and that perhaps Edward should start wearing a shirt and tie in order to bring himself up to Honey's standard.

He came out of his consulting room one afternoon to find her standing by Ginny's desk, cradling a young month-old baby in her arms.

'Little Imogen is simply gorgeous,' Honey told Carrie, Imogen's mother, before cooing at the baby, 'And now that we're sorting out your colicky problems, you'll be even more irresistible.' She pressed her lips to the baby's bald head, kissing her lightly. 'Yes, you will, sweetheart. So precious. So special. I'll bet your Mummy and Daddy can't stop kissing you.'

'You're right,' Carrie remarked. 'Even though she hasn't been well, she's still our angel.'

Honey smiled and sighed as she handed Imogen back to her mother and Edward could see a secret yearning in Honey's eyes. He knew she yearned that one day her wishes would come true and she'd find a place where she felt at home, where she could stay for ever and raise her family. Children. Honey had made no secret that she wanted children.

Edward shook his head and disappeared back into his consulting room, closing the door behind him, blocking his attractive colleague from view. He was determined to maintain a controlled distance with her given they both wanted different things from life. Even though he was incredibly drawn to her, like a moth to the flame, Honey was looking to settle down and have children, and whilst he may not know exactly what he wanted to do once Hamilton finally left the nest, he knew for certain he didn't want children. He'd done his time. That part of his life was over.

Still, that hadn't stopped him from wanting to spend

time with her, to chat with her, and when Hamilton had suggested one night that they ask Honey to join them for dinner, Edward had jumped at the chance.

'Small-town manners,' he'd told himself as he'd walked to the coach house and knocked on the door. 'It's polite to ask her to join us for a meal,' he'd muttered, waiting for her to answer. He'd knocked again, wondering if she was in the shower, but after a few more minutes of waiting he'd walked around to where her car was usually parked and found it gone. She wasn't home. The deflation of his spirits couldn't have been faster than that of a balloon losing air.

The following morning when he bumped into her in the kitchenette, he casually enquired as to her whereabouts the previous evening and she'd laughingly told him that, apart from her first night there, she'd been invited out every night to someone's place for dinner.

'It's so lovely,' she told him. 'Everyone is making me feel so welcomed. I'm quite overcome.'

He had to admit she had been warmly welcomed by the community and he was pleased people weren't giving the new locum a difficult time. In fact, Honey seemed eager to fit in. She'd definitely adhered to his wishes of offering only traditional medicine to his patients and he'd seen no more of her hippy clothes around the clinic rooms.

Edward leaned against his desk, now wondering if he hadn't made an error in judgement, especially when she looked so dynamic and stunning in the feminine business suits she wore every day. Perhaps he should let her dress however she wanted, for either way she seemed to be driving him crazy.

Honey let herself into the coach house, pleased that for tonight at least she hadn't been invited out to dinner. The community at large had been incredibly welcoming but even she needed a break, a bit of time for herself.

She'd done well to follow Edward's stipulations for working at the clinic, dressing sensibly and only offering 'normal' medical treatment to the patients, but this afternoon when Mrs Etherington had popped in to report a vast improvement in her arthritic pain, Honey had been pleased and handed over the recipe so Mrs Etherington could make the special cream at home.

'It's just a recipe, after all,' she told herself as she slipped out of her suit and into a cotton T-shirt and loose, flowing skirt. She was about to settle down to some beans on toast and some research reading for her PhD. when she heard deep male voices, locked in battle, coming from the main house.

The anger in their tones made her wince inside and never being a person who could put up with loud confrontations, without another moment's hesitation she quickly reached for an empty cup and headed over. Eavesdropping had never been her style. Honey preferred to tackle whatever was happening head on, if she could, but as she came closer to the house, she couldn't help but overhear what was being said.

'I don't understand why I need to finish school. It's almost positive I'll get picked to play sport. The talent scouts have been at school all week,' Hamilton yelled.

'You are not throwing away your education *just* to play sport,' Edward yelled back.

Honey knocked loudly on the door, waited a second then opened it, surprised to find the door opening straight into the kitchen, a large wooden table off to the side, eight chairs around it. 'Hi. It's only me.' She held out the empty cup. 'I've run out of sugar and forgot to pick some up at the store after clinic ended.'

Both Goldmark men looked at her, Hamilton's face all red and hot with a belligerent gleam in his eyes. Edward looked a little embarrassed, arms crossed defensively over his chest, reminding her of the first morning they'd met. The atmosphere in the room was so thick she could have sliced through it with a blunt scalpel.

'I can get it if you just tell me which cupboard contains the sugar and then the two of you can go back to fighting. I have headphones. I promise I won't hear a thing.' She walked towards the cupboards as she spoke and it wasn't until she'd opened the first one that Hamilton broke the silence.

'Honey, you can be our impartial judge,' he said, determined to plead his case to her.

'Don't go bringing Honey into this,' Edward retorted. 'Go to your room and finish your homework.'

'You never listen to me. I'm not a child any more,' Hamilton yelled, before stomping from the room.

'Then stop acting like one,' Edward called back. He shook his head and sat down at the table, burying his head in his hands. Honey put the cup down on the bench and walked towards him.

'Here.' She placed her hands on his shoulders, pleased when he didn't shy away. 'Just try to relax for a moment.'

'Ha!' The word was wrenched from him without humour but he dropped his hands and sat up straighter in the chair. 'Impossible to do with him around. Honestly, he's the stubbornest of the lot. So determined, so pig-headed— and if you say he reminds you of me, I'll have to ask you to leave.'

Honey bit her tongue.

'We *are* the same,' he continued as Honey's fingers carefully started to work at the knots that had turned into boulders, buried in his trapezius. 'I know that but that's also why I need to push him. He's capable of so much more than running around an oval, kicking a ball.'

'Then again…' Honey spoke softly, calmly, the way she had when she'd been massaging Lorelai's feet on her first day at work. Edward closed his eyes, allowing her ministrations and her soothing words to wash over him. 'How often do talent scouts come to schools to look for players? Come to schools that aren't in the major capital cities? You're not wrong, though,' she continued. 'Education is vitally important and will most certainly give him a greater range of options.'

'Yes. Exactly. See? You get it.' Edward could feel the tension starting to seep from his muscles, unable to believe just how tight his shoulders felt. Honey kneaded on in silence, Edward's thoughts started to drift and a few minutes later he felt her clever fingers coming up his neck to the base of his skull, where she applied small strokes. His head was lighter, his anger and frustration at Hamilton starting to float away.

'Just listen to my voice and know that everything is going to be all right. Everything will work out just fine and there will be no more yelling, no more confrontation. Things will be smooth and calm with Hamilton. Just listen to my voice. You're doing a great job, Edward. Just relax.'

Edward felt his lungs fill completely with air before he slowly exhaled, allowing all his tension to float away, just as Honey had suggested.

'That's it. Focus on your breathing. In and out. Nice and slow and steady.'

'What are you doing?' Hamilton asked from the doorway behind her, and Honey smiled as she looked at him.

'Just helping Eddie to release his tension. Why don't you come and join us?' She inclined her head towards the table, her smile welcoming. Hamilton did as she asked but sat almost at the opposite end of the table from his brother.

'Would you like a massage?' she asked Hamilton, but he quickly shook his head. 'You're like my brother. He hates them, too. Says they give him goose-bumps.'

Edward chuckled at that and Honey removed her hands and sat down, bridging the distance between the two brothers. 'So? Shall we talk? Hamilton, you go first.'

Edward opened his mouth to protest but Honey simply reached over and placed her hand on top of his. 'Edward will listen.'

He closed his mouth.

For the next hour the two brothers talked, with Honey mediating the discussion, her tone calm and controlled, which helped the conversation to stay civilised. By the end it was decided that should Hamilton be offered a position by the sport scout, then a family meeting would be held with their other brothers to discuss the pros and cons. In the meantime, Hamilton wouldn't continually argue about going to school and would apply himself to his homework.

'You're good at mediating,' Edward said after Hamilton had headed off to bed. 'Do you do it often?'

Honey smiled. 'No. Quite the opposite, really. I was usually the one who required the mediation. My poor brother would more often than not be the one sitting between myself and my parents, making sure both sides were heard.'

'You? A troublemaker?' Edward smiled at her but shook his head, as though he didn't believe it. 'Never.'

Honey laughed as she collected her empty cup from the bench. 'And now, Dr Goldmark, if you'll excuse me, I have some reading to do and an outing to plan.'

'Do you mean *our* outing on Saturday?'

'Yes.'

'Can you give me a hint?'

'Nope.' She grinned at him. 'Goodnight.'

She was at the door before he called her name. 'What about the sugar?'

Honey chuckled. 'What sugar? I don't need any sugar.' With that, she waved goodbye and headed out the door, leaving a smiling Edward in her wake, concerned about Saturday, highly appreciative for what she'd done and completely confused about his feelings for her.

# CHAPTER FIVE

BY THE time Saturday rolled around, Edward felt completely on edge. Honey had flatly refused to allow Lorelai to come into the clinic for the rest of the week, saying she was a quick study, had things completely under control and that Lorelai needed to rest. He had to admit she was true to her word and he had received comments from many patients about the wonderful Dr Honeysuckle.

'She gave me this special cream, one that she made up *herself*,' Mrs Etherington had said when she'd bumped into Edward at the general store. 'And it has been the only thing that's given me any relief from my arthritis *for years*. She says it's all natural and she gave me the recipe so I can make it up myself.'

The glee on Mrs Etherington's face had stunned Edward and he'd been hard pressed to recall a time when the woman had looked so happy. 'It's nice that she's not locked into doing things in just the traditional way,' the woman had continued, and for a split second Edward had wondered whether she was having a dig at him, but in the next instant Mrs Etherington had nodded. 'I'm happy to keep coming back and seeing Dr Honeysuckle for as long as she's here.' Then she'd patted his hand and said more softly, 'I think your mother would have liked her.'

Edward had been too stunned to say anything. When

he'd been a young boy growing up, he'd been afraid of brisk Mrs Etherington and never had he heard her speak so gently or so intently. He'd nodded and smiled and that had appeared to be enough for Mrs Etherington who'd finished paying for her purchases and headed out the door.

'She's right, you know,' Connie, the owner of the general store, had agreed. 'Greg and I went to see Dr Honeysuckle on Thursday because, you know, we're having trouble conceiving and stuff, and she not only recommended some herbal treatments but she was so...' Connie stopped and shrugged. 'I don't know. She just listened to me as though I were the only patient she had. It was as though I really mattered to her. She made me feel...'

'Special?' Edward had supplied, when Connie had seemed to be searching for a word.

'Exactly. It's not that I don't like you or Lorelai but I grew up with you guys and even now it sometimes feels a little weird...you know, talking to you about such personal things, but that Honey, well, she's a *real* honey.'

At the petrol station, in the pub, even down at the fishing wharf, the whole town seemed to be buzzing with praise for Dr Honeysuckle. No smirks, no sniggers, just down-to-earth respect for the new locum.

Edward knew he should be happy, should be relieved that everything was working out perfectly, but he was still on edge. He knew it had little to do with the way Honey was settling into the practice and more to do with where she was planning on taking him today.

Initially she'd arranged to meet him at midday, after morning clinic had finished, but given there were only two patients booked in and that Lorelai had insisted on seeing them, he was now due to meet her at eight o'clock—in fifteen minutes' time.

He sat at the old wooden kitchen table in his big family

home, the table where he'd eaten so many meals, drunk so many cups of coffee, made many difficult decisions. The familiarity brought him little comfort. It was all *her* fault. Being around Honey unnerved him. That much was obvious. The whole town seemed to have taken to her, his brother Peter had called him a few times to check to see that everything was going all right, and Lorelai was certainly singing Honey's praises, too. Wherever he turned, someone, somewhere was telling him how much they liked the new locum.

It was rare for the practice to have a locum. If they'd needed one before, it had usually only been for a few days—a week at most—whilst he and Lorelai had attended conferences. Honey was the first big, long-term change the practice had undertaken and she was certainly proving to be a success. He knew it was more than her simply being a great doctor, it was also her bright, easygoing manner, her personality. He should be jumping for joy, knowing his patients were happy with the change, especially as Oodnaminaby wasn't a town to easily accept change. He should be incredibly happy that things had worked out.

So why was it that ever since Honey Huntington-Smythe had arrived in his home town he'd had a constant headache? Why was it that he hadn't been sleeping properly? Why was it that just thinking about Honey— the way her hair fell about her shoulders, how her clothes, whether suits or the more bohemian look, which suited her infinitely better, seemed to highlight her incredible body, how her fresh, cinnamony-earthbound scent seemed to linger around him after she'd left his presence—made him feel so shaken up?

Edward closed his eyes and pinched the bridge of his nose. She seemed determined to encourage him to talk about his parents, although she hadn't said anything more

about the idea since their chat early on Tuesday morning…
when she'd caressed his body with her eyes and called him
sexy. Was it any wonder he was having trouble sleeping?

Amelia had never made him feel so raw, so exposed,
so primal and he'd been considering marrying her. What
did it mean when he couldn't stop thinking about a woman
who was obviously so wrong for him? Then there was the
way she'd helped him with Hamilton, the way she'd released the tension in his shoulders, making him feel renewed and refreshed. He'd realised afterwards that she'd
used the acupuncture pressure points and wondered if he
hadn't been a little harsh when he'd told her he wanted
none of that 'alternative' stuff practised at his clinic. To
that end, she should also be allowed to dress however she
felt comfortable because he'd noticed that as soon as she
arrived home from the clinic, she changed her clothes.

Oodnaminaby Family Medical Practice wasn't about
rules and regulations, that wasn't what his parents had intended. They'd intended it to be a practice where the doctors worked with the patients to find the best outcomes,
the best treatment, and he knew without a doubt that if
Honey's alternative remedies worked, why shouldn't the
patients try them? Mrs Etherington had certainly been
impressed and willing to give it a go.

Either way, it didn't change the fact that Honey had
come into his life and rocked his previously even-keeled
existence.

'Hello?' She knocked twice on the back door before
opening it and coming in. Edward quickly stood, almost
knocking the chair over, and shoved his hands into his
jeans pockets. 'Hey. There you are. All ready to go?'

He took in her attire of jeans, hiking boots and long-
sleeved top, a thick Aran jumper tied around her waist.
Apart from when he'd seen her in her colourful pyjamas

the other morning, it was the first time he'd seen her in anything but dresses or skirts and he had to admit she looked fantastic. Then again he was sure she could wear a garbage bag and still look amazing.

'I take it I'll be needing a thick jumper?'

Honey shrugged. 'Depends if you're partial to the cold. As I've spent the better part of my life either living on the beach or in the tropics, the cold and I are not the best of friends.'

'A beach baby?' Now, why did the image of Honey in a bikini suddenly pop into his mind?

Her tinkling laughter surrounded him. 'Give me a summer's day over a winter one any time.'

'We get some cold weather here,' he added, collecting a jumper from the closet by the back door where he kept his thick coats, gumboots and wet-weather gear.

'I know.' Excitement lit her eyes. 'A new experience for me. I can't wait.'

Edward wasn't too far away from her and when he looked down into her face he was astonished to discover her eyes were now a vivid shade of green. Just like the sea on a stormy day.

'Wow.' The word escaped his lips before he could stop it as he stared into her eyes. 'You look...different.'

'Good different or bad different?'

Edward swallowed, then licked his lips, completely hypnotised. 'Er...your eyes are so...green.'

Honey laughed and nodded at his reaction. 'Good different.' She took a step closer, pleased that he hadn't looked away. She liked it when he looked at her as he was now, as though she was the most beautiful woman he'd ever seen. She wanted so desperately to put her arms around his neck and urge his head downwards until his lips met hers but she knew there was no rushing a man like Edward. From the discussions they'd had, it was clear he needed some time to himself, some space to sort things out, some room to get his head together, and she was more than happy to give him whatever he needed.

'Green is supposed to be a soothing colour,' she added, forcing herself to look away. Self-control. This day wasn't about her and what she wanted, it was about Edward, and although he may be looking at her right now as though he really did want her, she also knew that moment would pass.

'So…' She stepped forward and just as she'd done on her first day in Oodnaminaby, Honey took his hand in hers. 'Ready?'

'For?'

'A bit of fun. We're taking my car and you're driving.'

'To where?'

'That's for me to know and for you to find out!'

An hour and a half later, Honey and Edward stood at the bottom of a chairlift. It had been enjoyable watching him drive her pink car along roads he knew so well.

'Why are we taking your car?' he'd asked when she'd handed him the keys.

'Because I need to see how it handles on the mountain roads and as you drive them regularly, it seemed logical for you to be the one to drive.'

Honey had held her breath as she'd waited for his decision. He could have overruled her and demanded they take *his* car, to do things *his* way, that her plans for the day be brushed aside in favour of whatever *he* wanted to do. That was the way Kennedy had been.

'Fine.' Edward had accepted her keys and folded his six-feet-four-inch frame behind the wheel, loosening up as they drove along and in the end being quite impressed with the handling of her little car.

Now, as they looked up towards the top of the chairlift, Edward raised his eyebrows. 'This is your spontaneous idea? Walking up Mt Kosciuszko?'

Honey nodded, a large smile on her face as she took off the backpack she'd brought and handed their lift tickets to the attendant. 'It's a nice day, it's not too far from where you live and I confess I've always wanted to walk to the highest point of Australia.'

'So this is more about you than me?' Edward wanted to know, but Honey's only answer was a squeal of delight as she sat down next to him on the chairlift.

'Why should you get to have all the fun?' She waved brightly at the attendant. 'Thank you,' she called as Edward pulled the safety bar down across them, the weather gradually becoming cooler as they rose. 'It's exciting.'

'You're like a child at Christmas,' he remarked, unable to resist smiling back. Her excitement was infectious.

'How many times have you been up here?' she asked.

'On the chairlift to ski down, too many times to count. Walking from Ramshead Range to Mt Kosciuszko, only twice.'

Honey raised her eyebrows. 'And here I thought you'd be an experienced guide.'

Edward shrugged. 'My dad and I came up a week after my twelfth birthday. We walked up to the summit, took pictures and then headed to one of the camping areas where we pitched a tent for the night. Just the two of us, in the crazy Snowy Mountains weather. It was early December, which is of course summer here, and it was pretty cold overnight in that tent, but in the morning we woke to find ourselves surrounded by snow. It was incredible. It sparked a tradition and after that, every time one of my brothers turned twelve, dad would organise a camping trip when the weather was fairly safe, then he and the birthday boy would walk to the summit and tent it overnight.'

'What happened when the twins turned twelve? Did he take them together?'

'No. Each boy had their own special adventure.'

'He sounds like quite a man, your dad.' A pang of jealousy ripped through her. She wished her father had spent time with her. 'All I received when I turned twelve was a card stating I'd donated a chicken to a village in Africa. Not that that's a bad thing,' she quickly added. 'They needed the chicken more than I needed a gift, but it was still a little…'

'Disheartening for a twelve-year-old?' Edward ventured.

'Exactly. Anyway, tell me more about these camping trips. They sound fantastic.'

Their chair bounced up and down as they went through the first tower's sheaves, the calmness of the mountains surrounding them. Honey listened intently to everything Edward said, hearing the love and respect he carried for his father in his tone.

'Benedict was the last one to go on the birthday hike.' Edward paused, as though trying to control his emotions whilst relating the story. 'The next winter season was the year of the avalanche. The year my world changed. The year my parents died.'

Honey wanted to hold him, to touch him, to reassure him, to do anything she could to take away the pain and regret she could hear in his voice. The world about them was still, the sounds of the chairlift engines working in the distance, the coolness continuing to surround them.

'They were in Charlotte's Pass, doing house calls.' He shook his head, sadness and regret filling him. 'The avalanche came without warning and forty-three more people died that day. BJ was leader of the rescue team and Peter, who was only twenty years old, was a junior member, out on his first major job.'

Unable to contain her need to let him know that she was here to support him, Honey reached out and covered his hand with hers, giving it a little squeeze. She didn't want him to stop talking because she had a sense that he didn't discuss his parents' deaths all that often. She was also humbled he was doing it with her.

Edward turned to look at her, his voice shallow, his eyes filled with pain, regret and deep sadness. 'Poor Pete. So young to see such a sight.'

Honey nodded, trying to control her own emotions, blinking back the tears. One look at Edward's face and empathy had flowed through her. She squeezed his hand again, trying to be strong and supportive for him. 'Peter once told me that he grew up that day. It helped him to focus on what he really wanted to do with his life and now look at him, a national park ranger.'

Edward dragged in a deep, cleansing breath, unable to believe how incredible he felt saying this to Honey. Amelia had been in his life when the tragedy had struck. She'd offered her condolences, she'd stood beside him at the funeral, and once his parents had been buried she'd expected his life to carry on as planned. What she hadn't expected was all the 'baggage', as she'd termed his younger brothers, that had come with his parents' deaths.

Honey, however, hadn't gushed with emotion, she hadn't offered bland apologies for the tragedy that had struck his life. Instead she was supportive and uplifting. He'd seen her blink back the tears, he'd seen that she'd been affected by what he'd related and, even though she'd heard the story from Peter, her reaction to *his* words was just what he needed.

'That's Pete,' Edward agreed with a nod. 'Always seeing the glass as half-full rather than half-empty. So do you, Honey. No wonder you and Peter became friends.'

'You're like that, too, Edward.'

'No.' He instantly dismissed her words with a shake of his head. 'I'm far too pessimistic. I'm old and set in my ways.'

'You're thirty-two!' She chuckled. 'That's far from old and if you're so set in your ways, why are you riding up a chairlift and getting ready to walk to the highest point in the country?'

'Because you're making me?' he asked, a slight smile touching his lips, but she rolled her eyes and shook her head.

'No. It's because you're daring.'

He laughed at that. 'I am not daring, Honey.'

'I disagree. Don't you realise that in accepting full custody of your brothers, being the Rock of Gibraltar for your family and friends, supporting a community in a time of need, you've been more bold and daring than anyone I've ever met? You've shared experiences with your brothers that are unique and precious and I'll wager that on the whole the good times far outstrip the bad.' She squeezed his hand again, desperately wanting to show him that he *was* an incredible man. 'And I'll bet that three years after your parents' deaths it was you who brought twelve-year-old Hamilton up this very route so that he wouldn't miss out on his birthday camping trip. Am I right?'

'Pete told you, didn't he?'

Honey shook her head and blinked back the tears that were threatening to dash onto her lashes. 'No.' Little puffs of air came from her mouth as she spoke and she gave him a watery smile. 'You're a quiet achiever, Edward. A man who perhaps gives too much of himself to other people. How often do you stop to consider what *you* want from life? What are those deep thoughts you've pushed to the furthest reaches of your mind? You work and you work and you work. You get stuck in the day-to-day rut and it's easy to leave those deep thoughts out of sight, not stopping to think about them, but you have to. At some point, you just have to or those deep thoughts can turn poisonous and start to infect your life.'

'You sound as though you're speaking from experience,' he murmured, unable to believe how close to the truth she'd come.

'I am. It was the reason I studied psychology. I wanted to try and understand where my parents were coming from, to understand their rationale. When my mother was in her late forties, she became pregnant. She'd always struggled with pregnancies, saying that Woody and I were her little miracles. Yet she refused to have scans, to see a GP or even a midwife to check that everything was all right. She kept saying she could do it the natural way, that everything was fine.' Honey paused and shook her head. 'Everything wasn't fine. If she'd had her scans, if she'd had an amniocentesis, then she would have discovered the baby had a congenital heart defect. They could have delivered the baby at thirty-seven weeks and performed surgery to fix the problem but instead my mother wanted to do it naturally. As a result, my little sister lived for an hour before she died.'

'How old were you?'

'Almost eighteen. I couldn't believe their blinkered view of the world. Things are not black and white, right or wrong, traditional or alternative. There needs to be a balance. I knew if I stayed with my parents, the poison in my mind would eat away at me. So, when I turned eighteen, I left. I went to live with my grandparents and over the years I was able to rationalise what happened. I started focusing on the simple things in life that make it so grand, such as helping my grandfather restore his old cars. Or going shopping with my grandmother, or hanging out with my brother and going to the movies. Or sitting on the beach at sunset.'

'Putting your arms out to the side and twirling around, absorbing the delights of the world?' he asked, recalling far too easily how beautiful she'd looked the first moment he'd laid eyes on her.

'Yes. Exactly. Those awesome, fun-filled, simple things that make life so worthwhile. That's what counts and I'm sure you have a plethora of memories, things you've shared with your brothers over the years.'

Edward nodded, remembering times when he and his brothers would roll around on the floor rough-housing, or when he'd come home late from an emergency to find eleven-year-old Hamilton had prepared baked beans on toast for dinner. If that was what was important in life then, yes, he'd had a terrific amount of those 'simple things' Honey was talking about. 'I have.'

She smiled at his words and let go of his hand as they were coming to the end of their chairlift ride. The attendant at the top helped them to disembark safely, Honey carrying the backpack as they walked passed the tall building that housed Australia's highest restaurant to the sign that indicated the different mountain walks.

'It's brisker up here.' She opened her backpack, pulling on a beanie and a pair of gloves. 'Here.' She handed over gloves and a beanie to Edward. 'I found these in the coach-house cupboard. I didn't want to give too much away about our destination so I packed them for you.'

Edward put them on. 'Worried that I'd refuse to come?'

She shrugged before putting the pack on, flatly refusing his offer to carry it for her. 'It doesn't matter now. You're here.' She smiled brightly, her earlier enthusiasm bubbling over once more. 'Come on. Let's get started. I can't wait to get to the top of Australia.'

'OK.' He peered out at the clouds. 'March is supposed to be the best month for walking up here but the weather can be very unpredictable. Here's hoping it won't give us any trouble today.'

They headed down the paved path before crossing a metal bridge, the small stream babbling along nicely, patches of ice visible here and there. In some areas around them were beautiful wild flowers, just starting to bloom. In other little valleys, where the sun didn't often reach, were patches of snow.

Honey oohed and ahhed at it all, pulling a camera from her pack and snapping photographs all around her. 'It's glorious,' she breathed as they reached the lookout. They'd passed a few other people along the way, most of them on their way down, others stopping to take photographs. There was an elderly retired couple, a family with three teenagers and a young couple, dressed warmly, the father carrying a toddler strapped firmly to his chest.

'Here. Let me take your photo,' Edward insisted, and Honey immediately struck a pose, laughing and changing position as he kept snapping.

'Now let's get one of both of us,' she said. 'To mark this auspicious occasion.' She drew closer to him, putting her arms about his waist, startling Edward so much he almost dropped the camera.

'No. I'll just take pictures of you.'

'Don't be silly. Quick. Hold your arm out straight and watch the birdie.' She smiled and held the pose. There was nothing more for him to do but to take the picture. 'There,' she remarked. 'That wasn't so bad, was it?'

They continued on, walking carefully on the raised metal-grate path that had been installed in order to protect the surrounding flora from being trampled. Edward had to admit things looked different from the time he'd walked up here with his younger brother. It had been a difficult trip for him, reliving memories of the time he'd walked the same path with his father. Hamilton had been oblivious, running on pure excitement which, in the end, had made the trip worthwhile.

When they finally reached the summit, they both stood there and breathed out at the rolling hills before them. 'We did it!' Honey stood on top and twirled around, her arms out wide. Edward quickly raised the camera and took several pictures. Although she was dressed in jeans, boots and Aran jumper, the beanie, gloves and scarf she wore were bright and colourful, making her stand-out against the backdrop of granite rocks with tufts of grass here and there, blue sky above.

She laughed and stopped spinning, turning to smile up at him. They were at the highest point in the country and they were all alone. When she looked at him like that, his gut tightened with desire. Good heavens, she was beautiful. Her cheeks were brisk and rosy from the walk, her red lips enticing as she smiled, and her eyes glowed bright with excited delight.

'Let's have our picnic,' she said, pulling off her gloves, stuffing them into her jeans pocket and opening her backpack. Within five minutes Edward was sitting on a rug, sipping a hot mug of coffee and eating a sandwich.

'If someone had asked me earlier this morning where

I'd be eating lunch, I wouldn't have had any idea it would be at the top of Australia.' Edward bit into his sandwich and chewed, seemingly completely satisfied.

'That was the general idea.' Honey swallowed her mouthful. 'Do you know, you can shout anything up here.'

'Shout?'

'Sure. You can go really bizzonkers.'

'Bizzonkers?' He raised an eyebrow as she stood and turned her face into the breeze. The weather was starting to change again, to become cooler, but she loved the briskness.

'Yep. You can shout anything into the wind. It doesn't even have to make sense. Watch.' Honey took a deep breath and cupped her hands around her mouth. 'Hey, everybody, it's time to walk your fish and milk your moose. Woo-hoo.'

Edward laughed at what she was saying, admiring her lack of inhibition. It was *that* quality which was drawing him in.

She took another deep breath and yelled again. 'Standing here, I feel complitified.'

'Com-what?' Edward finished his sandwich and headed to stand next to her.

'Complitified,' she said in her normal tone, brushing a stray strand of hair out of her mouth and tucking it beneath her beanie. 'It means you're completely verified.'

'You just made that up.'

'That's the point. You try it.'

'*You're* bizzonkers,' he muttered with a laugh, her silly word tingling on his tongue.

'Sure am. Now it's your turn. Take a deep breath and yell anything you want.'

'No.'

'Go on, Edward. You'll feel complitified afterwards. I promise.'

'I'll be fine,' he remarked, and bent to start packing the food away.

'Edward.' Honey reached for his arm and tugged him up, hoping he wouldn't fob her off. She could tell he was resisting because it was a big step outside his comfort zone but deep down inside she knew if he gave her a firm and resounding 'no', she'd stop. Kennedy had said no whenever she'd suggested something that little bit different or daring and in the end he'd tried to repress who she really was. It was one of the reasons why she was determined to try and be exactly who she was right now, and she desperately wanted Edward to free himself too.

'Come on. Just yell something. It's all part of doing something crazy, something different, something no one expects you to do. Let go. Be free. Achieve emancipation!'

Edward looked down at her, knowing she wasn't going to let this go. If there was one thing he'd learned about Honeysuckle Huntington-Smythe this week, it was that she was a highly determined woman.

'Fine.' He turned his face to the wind, feeling the first sprinkling of mist pass over. It felt fresh, it felt new.

'Hold your arms out,' she encouraged, a thrill passing through her at his acceptance.

He did as she suggested and tried to think of something to say. He frowned.

'Don't think too hard, Edward. Just yell the first thing that comes to mind.'

He nodded, then closed his eyes as though he couldn't believe what he was about to do. He took a deep breath, then yelled, 'Coffee tables can't sing karaoke.'

Honey was delighted, laughter bubbling up within her. 'Brilliant. Do another one,' she urged.

Edward's smile tugged at his lips as he thrust his arms even wider to the side. 'Coconuts look good in red nail polish!'

Edward couldn't believe how free he felt. It was as though yelling ridiculous things into the wind, as though not caring about what anyone else thought had lifted an enormous burden from his shoulders. He looked at Honey and felt incredibly grateful she'd brought him here today. If she'd told him where they were going, he might have baulked about coming to Mt Kosciuszko given the memories he'd shared with his father. Right now, though, he knew that had his father been alive, had his father come with them on this trek, he would be turning his face into the wind and yelling things no doubt more ridiculous than Edward could imagine. It made him feel closer to the memory of his father.

'That's it,' she encouraged.

He did another. 'Yelling into the wind at this altitude is making me light-headed.'

'Hey, that one made sense,' she protested. 'But I'll let it slide because it's also very true.' The wind was starting to increase, swirling around them, and not too far off they could see mist heading their way. She put her arms out wide and yelled, 'This place is awesome. I love being in the clouds.' Then turned to look at Edward. 'And I've enjoyed sharing it with you,' she finished in her normal tone. 'Thanks for trusting me, Eddie.'

He nodded, just looking at her, drinking her in, liking very much what he saw. Standing there in her bright scarf and beanie, stray strands of hair sneaking out to tickle the side of her face, she looked glorious. 'You keep calling me, Eddie.' His tone was deep, thick with repressed desire, and Honey found it completely addictive.

She took a small step closer. 'Tell me to stop and I'll never do it again.'

He didn't utter a word. Instead, he reached out and picked up the ends of her scarf and tugged her closer. He didn't know if it was because they were alone on the highest peak in the country or whether his light-headedness was affecting his otherwise rational judgement, but right now he wanted to know what it felt like to have that hypnotic mouth of hers pressed against his.

He had thought about her perfect lips throughout the week. Every moment he spent with her made him feel knocked off balance. He couldn't deny that there was a definite attraction pulsating between them, intensifying the more he tried to fight it.

'Why are you...?' he started to ask but stopped, his breath mingling with hers as he continued to look into her upturned face. 'You're so beautiful, Honeysuckle. I don't understand how you can still be single.'

Honey hesitated and, for a brief moment he saw sadness and pain reflected in her bright eyes. So there had been someone and something had gone wrong, causing her pain. A surge of protective energy shot through him at the thought of anyone hurting this incredible woman and he had to stop himself from gathering her close to his chest and never letting her go. The emotion felt right yet he knew it shouldn't.

She cleared her throat and gently shrugged one shoulder. 'Never found the right man. How about you? Why are you still single?'

'Never found the right woman,' he returned, and her lips tilted upwards at the edges.

'An amazing man like you?'

'An amazing man who upon the death of his parents gained custody of his younger siblings,' he returned pointedly, edging her even closer, his hands sliding up her scarf as though ensuring she wouldn't turn and walk away at his words.

'Ahh.' Honey nodded, pleased he wanted her near. 'Were you engaged?'

'We had discussed marriage.'

'She couldn't handle the thought of instant motherhood?'

'No. Her career was far too important.'

'She was a fool to let you go.' She slipped her arms around his waist and leaned into him even further.

He bent his head, now almost desperate to have his lips pressed firmly to hers, to taste and to experience the perfect flavours he knew her perfect mouth would provide.

This was it. Edward was going to kiss her. Honey could tell. She could see it reflected in his eyes as he looked from her mouth to her eyes and then back again. Her tongue slid out to wet her lips in an involuntary action of nervous anticipation. She rested her hands on his hips and rose up on tiptoe, angling her head back in order to close as much distance between them as possible.

His lips were almost there…almost…almost… And at the split second that she felt the slightest, most tantalising pressure of his lips against hers, the heavens above them opened up and the rain poured down.

'Quick!' Edward called, and both of them turned to pack up the remains of their picnic, the rug almost being blown away. Honey pulled two lightweight waterproof ponchos from the pack and they quickly helped each other to put them on. Edward insisted on taking the backpack and Honey was in no mood to argue.

'Let's head back. Chances are it won't be so bad fifty metres down the track,' Edward called near her ear, before taking her gloved hand in his. Honey more than willing for him to play the role of big strong hero. Besides, he knew the erratic weather in this part of the country far better than she did so it seemed only right that he be in charge.

They made slow but steady progress, visibility often reduced to about five metres in some of the small valleys. The entire time, though, Edward kept a firm hold of Honey's hand. 'Slow and steady is definitely going to win this race today,' he remarked as they continued.

'You know, Eddie, you don't have to make conversation with me to keep me calm or to slow me down. I love walking in the rain and being up this high. We're literally in the clouds. I have no objection to slow and steady,' she continued, her tone holding a hint that she wasn't only talking about the weather surrounding them. Edward cleared his throat but tightened his grip on her hand, deciding to ignore the double entendre.

'Even though you're practically soaked through?'

Honey's laughter mixed with the clouds swirling around them. 'Absolutely.'

'You are so different from the women I know.'

'Yeah?' She certainly hoped that was a good thing.

'Yeah,' he replied. They kept walking, hand in hand, treading carefully on the wet and slippery metal-grate path. They were heading downhill now and one slight error could cause them both to tumble.

The visibility started to increase so they could see a little further ahead.

'It's so quiet and still and peaceful and scary and exhilarating and I'm having so much fun.' Honey continued to step carefully but Edward could almost feel the excitement of their situation zinging through her gloved hand. 'I'm walking in a cloud. Another thing to cross off my bucket-list.'

'Bucket-list?'

'You know, the things you want to do before you "kick the bucket", before you die.'

'I know what a bucket-list is, Honey. I guess I just hadn't expected someone like you to have one.'

Honey glanced up at him very briefly but returned her gaze to the path beneath their feet. 'Someone like me?'

Edward was surprised he could detect the teasing note in her tone. 'I just meant you seem to live every moment to the fullest.'

'I *try* to. Sometimes I don't succeed,' she called, the wind starting to pick up around them, the visibility decreasing again. They were already talking fairly loud but as there was no one around, it didn't matter.

They came to a small valley where Mt Kosciuszko and Rams Head met. Edward squeezed on her hand, urging her to stop walking. Honey wasn't sure why they'd stopped and was about to ask him what was going on when he tugged her close, ignored the rustling of their wet ponchos and quickly dipped his head to capture her cold lips with his. Not a brief brush kiss this time. His lips lingered tantalisingly on hers, with the promise of so much more.

# CHAPTER SIX

KISSING Honey was like receiving manna from heaven and he drew her body closer to his, annoyed both of them were dressed in weatherproof ponchos, gloves and beanies. He wanted to run his fingers through her long and silky hair; he wanted to nibble at that delectable neck he'd caught glimpses of during the week. He wanted to have her arms wrapped around him as he took his sweet time exploring the wonders of this extraordinary woman.

Kissing her now had been a spur-of-the-moment thing, completely spontaneous, and while he was the type of man who for years, had meticulously planned everything, standing here with his mouth pressed firmly against Honey's he couldn't deny the appeal of following through on a thought.

He'd wanted to kiss her—so he had.

'Nice,' she said against his mouth, drawing the word out slowly, savouring it. 'Who knew the simple touch of your mouth to mine would be so incredibly...dynamic?'

Edward murmured his agreement, then closed his eyes and kissed her again, wanting to commit every shared sensation to memory. He'd locked his own wants and needs away for so long but now he'd broken the drought, so to speak, he wanted to continue sampling her sweet, flavoursome lips.

It felt right holding her in his arms, even though they were encumbered by wind, rain and plastic ponchos. Something deep within him felt as though it were breaking open, a crack in the armour he'd surrounded himself with for so long while he did what had to be done. It was as though freedom was close at hand, that his reward was near, that his life would soon start to make sense. He'd be able to walk his own path, rather than following the footsteps of others.

And Honey? Did she fit into that new world of freedom he'd been searching for? Was she merely the gatekeeper to show him the way? To put him on the right path? Was there room for her to walk along beside him? The thoughts jolted Edward back to the present, his mind zinging with possibilities, probabilities and a ton of questions.

He savoured Honey's addictive lips one last time, before pulling back, the wind having changed direction, the rain urging them to keep moving.

'I'm happy to continue exploring every contour of your lovely face…' He exhaled slowly, then glanced around at their present surroundings. 'But I fear now is not the time.'

'Or the place,' she added as he took her hand in his once more.

'Let's get to somewhere drier,' he suggested, and together they headed back onto the track. The rain had eased, the atmospheric disturbance having calmed down somewhat, and visibility was better.

Honey was elated because Edward had just kissed her. There had been no build-up, no shuffling dance towards each other. Edward had simply pulled her close and kissed her. Right out of the blue! She'd hoped that by bringing him here today, he'd have the opportunity to relax, to take some time out for himself, to do what *he* wanted to do. She smiled to herself. Edward had wanted to kiss her—

so he had. The knowledge warmed her heart faster than any heater.

'One more kilometre to go and we'll be back at the restaurant.' He stopped and looked over his shoulder, the path they'd walked along obscured by cloud. 'Do you want to take any more photographs now the weather is clearing up?'

'That's all right,' Honey replied, knowing the camera was stowed safely in the backpack. 'I've been taking plenty of mental snapshots and my memories are more reliable than any mere photograph. Plus, I can remember far more with my senses. I can remember the feel of the wind and the rain; the excited apprehension of being up so high; the sight of those clouds whirling around before covering us like a big white blanket and...I can remember the glorious taste of your lips against mine.'

She stood on tiptoe and brushed an extremely brief but highly tantalising kiss across his lips. 'Thank you for sharing this with me.'

Edward's mouth was still tingling from her touch and he swallowed. 'You knock me off balance, Honey. It's new and exciting and believe me when I say that I like it but it's all mov—'

A loud, blood-curdling scream filled the air and both Honey and Edward turned their heads, looking in the direction of the noise.

'What on earth was that?' she asked as they both stepped off the metal-grate path, being careful as they walked across the cushion plants and herbfield. The area around them was nowhere near as steep as it had been before but on both sides of their path were granite boulders and rocks, jutting out here and there. The ground was uneven but as they continued to walk in the direction of the scream, they heard more cries.

'Help. Help. Somebody—*help*!' It was a woman's voice and, judging from the direction, they couldn't be too far away.

'Just behind that stand of rocks.' Edward pointed with his free hand, his other one firmly holding onto one of Honey's.

'We're coming,' Honey called back. 'Where are you?'

'Over here,' the voice said from behind the rocks, just as Edward had indicated. 'Help me. Please. It's my son. He needs help.'

'We're on our way. Just keep talking,' Honey encouraged.

'What sort of supplies do you have in the backpack, Honey?' Edward asked as they drew closer to the woman's voice.

'Just a small, very basic first-aid kit. Sticking plasters, crepe bandages, disinfectant, triangular bandage and two small gauze pads. Oh, and some paracetamol. That's it.'

'Is there still some water left in the water bottle?'

'About half.'

'Over here,' the woman kept calling. 'Help me, please. My son's hurt.'

'Is he conscious?' Honey asked, as she allowed Edward to help her scramble over the rocks before them.

'No. Well, I don't know. I can't tell. Leonard? Leonard? Talk to me. Talk to me, please!' The woman's voice was starting to become hysterical just as Edward and Honey rounded the rocks. It was only then that Edward let go of Honey's hand, both of them quickly rushing to where a boy of about fifteen lay in an unconscious tangled position on the gravel at the base of the rocks. Honey recognised him as part of the family they'd passed when they'd been heading up to the summit.

'I'm Honey. This is Edward. We're both doctors.'

'Doctors.' The woman clutched her hands to her chest. 'Oh, thank you for stopping.'

'What's your name?' Honey asked the mother as Edward performed a quick assessment on the unconscious Leonard.

'Penny. Is he going to be OK? He was taking photographs and he…well, he just slipped. He was on his way down. I'd already told him to get down,' Penny commented, her words running over each other in her haste to get them out. 'He likes taking photos. Even saved up all his birthday and Christmas money to buy the camera.' Penny looked down at the smashed camera nearby. 'Now it's broken.' The woman choked on her words, clearly distressed by the situation and probably wondering whether her son was as badly broken as the camera.

Honey stood, crossed to where Penny was standing and put her hands on the woman's shoulders. 'It's all right. We're going to help Leonard and you can help him too by staying nice and calm.'

'Honey, I need you,' Edward called, and Honey crossed back to his side. He'd already retrieved the small first-aid kit from the backpack and had pulled off his gloves. The rain was starting to disappear now, heading off to swirl around on the other side of the ranges, but Honey had a feeling it would be back. If there was one thing she'd learned during her week in Oodnaminaby, it was that if you didn't like the weather, you only had to wait about fifteen minutes and it would change.

'What can I do?' She knelt down on the other side of Leonard. In essence, it was the first time she and Edward had worked together but both of them knew what needed to be done and had the skills to see it through. Edward was calling to Leonard, trying to see if the boy would respond, but to no avail.

Edward looked at their patient. 'Carotid pulse is strong, which is a good sign and indicative of no internal bleeding, respirations are conducive to head trauma.' As he pointed to Leonard's head, Honey noticed some blood on Edward's fingers. 'Head wound to the right side of the cranium just above the temporal pulse, possibly two centimetres in length. I don't want to move him any more at this point in order to confirm. Right leg is at an odd angle, possibly fractured at either the acetabulum or femur or both; right radial pulse is intermittent indicative of a possible radial or ulna fracture.' Edward extended his hand as he spoke. 'No doubt he put his hand out to help stop his fall.'

'Good heavens,' Penny mumbled, her trembling fingers covering her mouth as she stood by and listened to Edward's report. 'Is he in any pain? Oh, my poor boy.'

Edward looked up at the mother. 'He's unconscious, Penny, but he's breathing well. His airways aren't blocked and from what I could see when I lifted his eyelids, his pupils were the same size and reacted to the light.'

'Is that good?'

'It means the possibility Leonard has suffered any brain damage is minimal.'

'Brain damage?' Penny looked down at her supine son, fresh tears gathering in her eyes. Honey stood and put her hands on Penny's shoulders again.

'Penny. Look at me.' Honey's voice was soft but direct. When Penny finally lifted her eyes from her injured son, Honey smiled reassuringly. 'Where is the rest of your family? Does anyone else know about this accident? Have they gone to raise the alarm?'

Honey was fairly sure she knew the answer, given she and Edward had been the only two people walking on the path and hadn't seen anyone else after they'd heard Leonard's scream.

'N-no. Oh, no! Howard will be so cross. He didn't want Leonard to come over this way, to leave the path, but Leonard wanted to take some photos. He does a class at school. He's very good but Howard doesn't understand and all they do most of the time is fight,' she explained as she wrung her trembling hands. 'I told him to take the younger two children back to the chairlift and that I would get Leonard and follow them down. I couldn't find him at first but, just before we were engulfed in the misty rain, I found him. He was on the rocks, taking photographs of the clouds rolling in. I begged him to get down, to hurry up…and…' she hiccuped '…that's when he…he jumped.' New sobs peppered her words. 'Oh, Howard's going to be so cross when he finds out.'

'Do you have a phone on you?'

'Yes.' Penny looked hopeful. 'I forgot about my phone. How silly is that?'

'Not silly at all,' Honey reassured her. 'You were focused on Leonard.'

'There should be fairly strong phone reception,' Edward interjected. 'There's a cellphone base station at the restaurant and as we're not that far away, the signal should be strong enough to call for help.'

'Oh, good. Yes. I'll call Howard,' Penny said as she dug through the layers she was wearing in search of her phone, her tone much calmer now.

'Call emergency services first.' Honey told Penny the number to dial. 'Ask for the paramedics, tell them we're approximately one kilometre from the restaurant.' Honey knelt down to help Edward with getting Leonard as stable as they could. Edward had applied some sticking plasters to the minor areas where Leonard had sustained a few cuts and was presently bandaging the right arm.

'Radial pulse has improved. Vital signs still good. I've

just placed one of the padded bandages beneath his head where I could see the cut in order to provide some pressure to stem the bleeding. As far as his leg goes, I don't have a clue what to use as a splint.'

Honey looked around them. 'We're above the tree line. There are only rocks, no branches.' She thought quickly, mentally working through what was in her backpack. 'I have a couple of books in there—just small ones but enough to supply a bit of stability until the paramedics arrive.'

'You brought books with you on our date?'

'Hey, this isn't a date, Eddie. When we go on a date, you'll know about it.'

Edward glanced at her and couldn't help smiling at the way she was all fire and determination. The more he discovered about Honey, the more he liked what he found. She was a clear thinker, resourceful and able to think outside the box. It was true that since his break-up with Amelia he hadn't even bothered to try dating again. Raising Benedict and Hamilton and stabilising the family practice had been his main concerns, and paying for Bart to go to medical school. He'd been left with little time for dating.

Now, though, things were different. Things had changed. Benedict was now at medical school and Hamilton was in his final year at school. Edward had the time to date and, lo and behold, along came Honey, the most flamboyant, humorous and sensual woman he'd ever met. She was so incredibly different from Amelia, from the sort of woman he'd always thought he would end up marrying, that it was no wonder she'd made such an impact.

She was by no means traditional in her approach to life; she most certainly didn't have a boring sense of style and her personality…well, he couldn't shake the feeling that in helping him to step out of his very comfortable comfort zone, she was showing him how vibrant life could be. Plus, he had to admit, seeing the world through Honey's eyes—standing on the highest mountain, with his arms back, yelling ridiculous things into the wind—had been incredibly liberating as well as a lot of fun.

Kissing her had been equally so.

He looked at the woman kneeling beside him as they worked together to get Leonard as comfortable as they possibly could. Penny had managed to phone through to the emergency services and, with their help had relayed information about their current position and what injuries Leonard had sustained. Once that was done, Penny took a deep breath and called her husband, Howard, letting him know the situation.

Edward and Honey splinted Leonard's leg with the books, which Edward discovered were two paperback books about the history of the Snowy Mountains area. Honey pressed her fingers to the boy's tibial pulse.

'Blood is flowing much better now that it's splinted,' she reported.

'Good.' Edward took Leonard's vital signs again, pleased with the outcome. 'He's as stable as we can get him. Now we just need to wait for the paramedics.'

'How long should that take?'

'About an hour,' he replied as they covered Leonard with the rug they'd used for their picnic. 'Given his clothes are wet, we need to ensure he stays as warm as possible.'

'Agreed. Let's wrap my scarf carefully around his neck to act as a soft cervical collar. If only I'd packed a magazine or something.'

'First books, now magazines. Did you think you were going to get bored, coming out with me?' Edward asked, and Honey gave him a quizzical look, detecting a veiled hurt beneath his words.

'Has that happened to you before? Have you been out on a date only to have a woman prefer the company of her book to you?'

Edward's eyes widened at her words. 'How did you...?' He stopped, looked down at Leonard as they carefully secured the scarf in place to protect the spine, then back at Honey again. 'Yes, but in my defence, I was only nineteen at the time.'

Honey shook her head disgusted with the unknown woman. 'It doesn't matter. No one should be treated that way and that woman was a fool. When we go out on *our* first date, I promise you my *full* attention.'

'You usually give everyone your full attention, no matter what you're doing. Whether it's your patients, or Ginny, or Brad at the service station, or Connie at the grocery store.'

'Have you been watching me?'

'I've been *told* about you, by so many people. You've really made an impression on the whole town, Honey.'

'I usually *do* make an impression on people,' she countered, but he could tell she was pleased. 'Whether or not it's a positive one is the debatable point.'

'Well, I can tell you it's all extremely positive.' He studied her for a brief moment. 'And I have to say I was wrong in asking you to dress more formally. You should feel comfortable when you're consulting and you always look nice in everything you wear.'

She raised her eyebrows. 'No more suits?'

'That's up to you. Also...' He paused, meeting her gaze. 'If you feel a patient will benefit from alternative means of treatment, then I have no objection. The massage you gave me the other night really helped to reduce my tension and I know you were using pressure points.'

Honey gave him a sheepish grin. 'Yeah. I was. I wasn't sure you'd notice but you…well, I thought you needed it. You were pretty stressed at the time.'

He nodded. 'I was but you diagnosed the situation quite accurately and applied the necessary remedy. It's clear you honestly care for the well-being of the patients and at the end of the day that's what matters most. You provide your expertise and you listen to them. That's special.'

'You're right,' she agreed. 'That's all every single person wants in life—for someone to listen to them. Not just half-heartedly but to really listen, to take what they say seriously, to understand what they might be going through or feeling.' She looked down at their patient as they once more performed observations, Honey helping Edward to change the pad beneath Leonard's head, both of them pleased the bleeding seemed to have stopped.

'Take poor Leonard here. It doesn't sound as though he gets on all that well with his father.' She inclined her head towards Penny, who was still talking on the phone, having put a bit of distance between them. 'And the expression on Penny's face tells me she's a little scared of her husband. No doubt Howard has his own set of problems, just as we all do, but if everyone simply stopped and really listened to the people who are the most important to them, chances are the world would be a lot nicer to live in.'

'Who do you talk to, then?' Edward asked.

'My brother. My grandparents.'

'Not your parents?'

She shook her head. 'I haven't spoken to them in years.'

'You can't forgive them? Leave the past in the past?'

Honey shrugged. 'It's complicated.'

Edward shook his head. 'No, it's not, Honey. It's as simple as picking up the phone and saying "Hello". Do you have any idea just how much I'd love to be able to do just that. To speak to my parents one last time? Life's too short, Honey.'

She held his gaze for a moment before looking down at their patient, her mind whirring with his words. She picked up Leonard's left wrist to check his pulse. 'Pulse is strong. Leonard? Leonard?' She called to their patient. 'Can you hear me?'

This time, for the first time since one of them had called to Leonard during the course of treating him, they got a response.

'Mum?' It was only a slight murmur but it was such a good sound.

'Penny?' Honey called, and beckoned the mother over. 'He's starting to stir.'

'Oh. Oh.' Penny disconnected the call from her husband, even though he was no doubt in mid-bluster, and crossed to their side.

'He's still very groggy and you need to keep very calm when you talk to him. He needs to remain as still as possible and not to panic.' Honey glanced at her watch. It hadn't been all that long since the call had gone out and the only pain medication she'd brought was paracetamol. Still, it was better than nothing.

'The emergency call will be relayed to the first-aid team in Thredbo village and they're situated at the bottom of the chairlift,' Edward said to Penny. 'They'll come up first with the stretcher so hopefully by the time the ambulance arrives we'll have Leonard at the bottom of the mountain.'

'Leonard?' Penny called, bending down next to Honey. 'It's Mummy.'

'Mum?' The word was stronger now and Honey could hear the rising panic in the teenager's voice.

'Stay calm,' she said.

'You've had an accident,' Edward confirmed in his deep, authoritarian tone. 'I'm Edward and this is Honey. We're both doctors and we're looking after you,' he informed the teenager. 'We need you to lie very still until the stretcher arrives.'

Leonard went to nod his head but immediately cried out in pain.

'Keep very still, including your head,' Edward instructed again, placing his hands on either side of Leonard's head to steady him.

'Just look at your mum, sweetie. She's here for you. So are we. Everything's going to be just fine.' Honey's voice was soothing and calm. 'Just keep looking at your mum and know that everything will be all right.' She reached beneath the blanket for Leonard's left arm, quickly checked the pulse, pleased it was stronger than before, then stroked his arm a few times before applying pressure with her thumb to the inside of his wrist. 'Close your eyes. Know that you are loved, that you are cared for,' she continued, her tone almost hypnotic. 'Breathe easy. All will be well with your world.'

Leonard did as she said and the stress lines that had moments ago been evident on his face relaxed.

'That's it. Keep relaxing. Let your body heal. Everyone is looking after you and there is nothing for you to worry about. Your mum is here and she loves you very much. You're safe. You're wrapped in a cocoon of happiness, light and love.'

Leonard's breathing eased and his chest rose and fell as though he was relaxed and ready for a nice long sleep.

'Just keep talking to him in nice, calm tones,' Honey

said to Penny, not changing her tone. 'Relax him with your words. Reassure him everything will turn out fine and that you love him. Can you do that?'

Penny held Honey's gaze for a moment before nodding.

'Great. Here. Take his hand. Just hold it. Stroke it lightly. Let him feel your touch. Let him feel your love.'

Penny did as she was told and a moment later Honey stood and stretched out her muscles then looked down at Edward. She was surprised to find him watching her with that same quizzical expression she'd seen several times during the week.

'Did you just…hypnotise the patient?' His tone was filled with incredulity.

'No.' She smiled at him. 'I used the pressure point at the base of the wrist to help him relax. Pressure there, combined with a soothing and calm tone, can work wonders on someone who's been traumatised.'

Edward shook his head in happy bemusement. 'You are amazing, Honeysuckle. At every turn, you're intriguing me further.'

'Good.' Her shining green eyes were bright and alive with life. 'That's just the way I like it.'

# CHAPTER SEVEN

THANKFULLY, the first-aid team from Thredbo village came up with a stretcher and by the time the ambulance had arrived from Jindabyne, they'd managed to get Leonard safely back to the first-aid post, ready for his transfer to Cooma hospital.

'We can take it from here,' Sheldon, the paramedic, told Edward as the two men shook hands. 'Get back to enjoying your day away from the demands of patients.' Sheldon clapped Edward on the back before closing the rear doors of the ambulance and walking around to the driver's side. His partner, Raj, was safely ensconced in the back, monitoring Leonard's condition.

Penny's husband, Howard, and their other two children were going to follow in their car.

'Howard seems a lot calmer now,' Honey commented to Edward after both Howard and Penny had thanked them for their assistance.

'Perhaps he's starting to realise things could have been a lot worse.'

'Or perhaps he's thinking about whatever it was you said to him.' Honey looked up at the man beside her. 'I saw you having a quiet word with the blustering Howard while the paramedics were re-splinting Leonard's leg.'

Edward seemed self-conscious for a moment and

shrugged one shoulder. 'Life is too short to be blustering your way through it.'

'Is that what you told him?'

Edward's answer was to give another shrug as though he didn't like being in the spotlight, and Honey couldn't help but think he looked so cute when he did that. 'I may not have used those exact words, but—yeah, something like that.'

Honey leaned up and pressed a kiss to his cheek. 'You're a good man, Edward Goldmark.'

It wasn't the first time someone had said something like that to him and ordinarily it was the type of compliment that made him nod politely and move on to the next topic, but with Honey, the way she looked so intently into his eyes, the way his cheek still zinged with the sweet touch from her lips, the way she made him feel as though he was the only man who mattered in the world, caused his chest to swell with pleasure. The fact that Honey thought nice things about him mattered and while he knew he should probably be more concerned about that, he allowed himself to accept her heartfelt words.

'What's next on the agenda?' Edward needed to move things forward otherwise he'd probably spend all day dwelling on the way Honey made him feel and that would be of little use to anyone. He appreciated her bringing him out today and it hadn't been until he'd been on top of Mt Kosciuszko, yelling at the top of this lungs, that he'd started to realise just how tightly he'd been holding on to his life. Life was too short. Those were the words he'd said to Howard, to try and get through to the man just how lucky he was to have a wife and three children.

He glanced at the beautiful woman beside him, still struck by her generosity of spirit, how she was a giver, wanting others to feel the freedom of life she'd discovered.

Yet at times he'd seen glimpses of a woman who wasn't completely happy. She wanted permanence, to find a home where she belonged, but even while she was searching for her own place in this world, she didn't lock others out. She nurtured, cared, gave her time and experience to others at the drop of a hat and never asked for anything in return.

Medicine was a vocation to her, something vitally important that she *must* do in order to be true to herself. She didn't look upon it as a ladder-climbing career and, given her qualifications, she could well be head of a hospital department by now. She was quite a woman.

'Well, I had thought we might have a nice warm drink at the restaurant at the top of the chairlift but as we're now down the bottom—' Her words were cut off as Edward picked up her backpack and took her hand in his, heading back to the chairlift.

'Then that's what we're going to do.' Once more they rode the chairlift to the top, noticing some mountain-bike riders heading down the steep slopes. Another daredevil was sitting in the seat in front of them, holding his push-bike as the chairlift continued to rise, taking them back to the top of the mountain.

'They're crazy.' Honey laughed as she watched them speed down the almost vertical track.

'Crazy but well padded and very safety conscious. Peter and Bartholomew used to do this when they were younger.'

'But never you,' Honey stated.

'No.'

'Did you want to?'

Edward thought about it. 'Maybe. I recall being more jealous at the fact they actually had the time to do it. I was either away at medical school or, whenever I was home for Christmas, there was always studying to be done.'

'Did you never grasp the concept of all work and no play can make Edward a very stressed-out man?' There was humour in her tone but also a large amount of caring concern. She cared about him. He wasn't exactly sure why the thought should warm him so much but it did. 'And after medical school, you had a different life to live,' she continued.

'Yeah.'

'So I guess daredevil mountain biking was then out of the question.' She raised her eyebrows and sat up straight as though an idea had just occurred to her. 'You should definitely add it to your bucket-list, though.'

'I need a bucket-list now?'

'Well, if you don't want to have one, I'll put it on my list and we can do it together.' Excitement danced in her eyes, the thrill of adventure in her voice, and Edward could only smile, captivated by her inner beauty.

When they reached the top, they stepped from the chairlift and headed into the restaurant, glad of the warmth and homely atmosphere. They removed their wet-weather ponchos in the downstairs anteroom before heading upstairs.

'Oh, I'm so glad you came back up,' the restaurant's hostess greeted them as they entered. 'How did the young boy make out?'

'He'll be fine,' Edward said, and introduced Honey to Bernadette. 'We went to the same high school,' he told Honey.

'That's right.' Bernadette shook hands warmly with Honey. 'I was in the same year as the twins but even though Edward was a few years ahead, we all caught the same bus together every day.' She spread her arms wide, indicating a table for two. 'Now, both of you sit down and I'll bring you some drinks. Some nice hot cocoa to warm you up.'

And before either Edward or Honey could protest, Bernadette had disappeared behind the kitchen door.

'It's lovely up here,' Honey remarked, walking to the window to look out at the scenery. The clouds were moving again, rolling over the hills, the rain heading back in their direction. She breathed in, then caught a whiff of her Aran jumper. 'Oof, that's bad,' she remarked, and as Bernadette had lit a fire in the slow combustion heater, she removed the jumper and draped it over a chair. 'The jumpers keep you very warm but they don't smell the best when wet.' She rubbed her hands together and held them up to the fire.

'I think you smell gorgeous,' Edward remarked as he came to stand behind her, breathing in the cinnamony-earthy scent he was rapidly becoming addicted to. Honey felt warmth flood over her and it had nothing to do with the burning logs and everything to do with the heat radiating from Edward's close body. 'What *is* the name of your perfume?'

'I don't wear any.' Her tone was soft and she closed her eyes for a moment, wanting to absorb the exciting tingles that flooded down her spine and spread throughout her body as his breath fanned close to her ear.

'Impossible. You always smell incredible.'

'I do?' Honey was surprised at his compliment. It wasn't something she'd expected him to come right out and say but it appeared Edward was really starting to loosen up and she wasn't about to look a gift horse in the mouth.

'Distractingly so,' he admitted quietly, the heat from his nearness causing her cheeks to flush.

She shrugged and opened her eyes, turning to glance up at him, her shoulder brushing against his chest. She gasped at the connection. Pure masculine heat flowed from him through her, making her body tingle from the tips of her hair right down to her toes. Didn't Edward have any idea just how much he could affect her? That she was highly susceptible to his charms?

She'd been looking for *her* place in the world for some time now but she'd been looking at towns and people and houses. She hadn't been looking for a man. 'How do you know when you're in love?' she'd once asked her grandmother. Jessica had looked over to where Hubert had been reassembling the manifold of an old classic car, grease accidentally smeared on his face here and there. Her eyes had twinkled and she'd sighed peacefully. 'You just know, dear.'

Honey glanced at Edward once more, her heart doing flips of happiness at being so near him, her stress and tension ebbing away simply because he was there. 'Er... well...I use honeysuckle soap.'

'Honeysuckle soap?' he asked, trying to keep himself under control. She was close, she was almost leaning into him and, with the memory of their previous kisses still fresh in his mind, it was difficult to control the urge to simply bend his head and capture her glorious mouth once more.

'Well, quite a few honeysuckle things. It's like a little joke between me and my brother,' she continued, surprised her mind could even form words given the way her body was jumping for joy at this direct attention from Edward.

'And?' he encouraged, watching the way her lips formed words when she spoke, her soft tone soothing him. Deep down inside, he felt at war within himself, wanting to draw her close but knowing he needed to push her away. His life was too emotionally scattered at the moment, especially after standing at the top of the world and yelling his stress away...but he couldn't help wanting to know more about the woman beside him. 'You can't just leave it there. You have to explain further.'

'It's nothing major, Edward. Just a bit of fun.' When he raised his eyebrows in question she rolled her eyes, loving the way neither of them wanted to move. Instead they seemed intent on prolonging the conversation simply so they had an excuse not to shift. 'OK, then. My brother has always given me anything honeysuckle scented—all natural products, nothing artificial. Soap, shampoo or conditioner, or scented oil or hand cream—whatever he can find, whenever he can find it. He even once bought me honeysuckle-scented furniture polish—which does nothing for the complexion,' she joked. 'And I have quite a few candles as well. Woody recently told me that he'd found honeysuckle-scented lip balm in Tarparnii. Lip balm.' She shook her head as though this astounded her. 'So you see, it's just silly but I do love the scent.'

'It suits you.' He nodded with approval, his tone soft, deep, intimate. There was nothing artificial about the woman before him. She was definitely *au naturale* and he appreciated every part of her. 'The scent. The name. You *are* Honeysuckle.' Their gazes met and held and she licked her lips, unable to believe how aware she was of the mounting tension between them.

'Thank you, Eddie.' She was surprised at the huskiness of her voice but didn't bother to clear her throat. She was more than willing for him to realise she was as affected by him as he appeared to be by her. 'What a sweet thing to say.'

'I'm a sweet guy,' he murmured, his face completely straight, and Honey couldn't help the smile that touched her lips. It only made her look more irresistible. Edward's heart seemed to be pounding against his chest, the blood pumping faster around his body, his need for this woman mounting each time he was near her.

He swallowed and her gaze dipped to his neck, following the action of his Adam's apple. She licked her lips as though she wanted nothing more than to press tantalising butterfly kisses to his skin, gradually working her way up towards his mouth. He clenched his jaw. He wanted that, too.

'Uh…' She lifted her gaze back to his.

'Hmm?' His eyes were hooded and Honey could clearly read the desire evident in the brown depths. Her heart was beating so fast and her breathing had become so shallow, she thought she might hyperventilate simply from being near Edward. She swallowed. 'Uh…I think we should…' She forced herself to close her eyes, severing the connection.

Honey knew Edward needed to move slowly. He might be fine to admit the attraction here, on top of the world, so to speak, but it would be a different story once they arrived back in Oodnaminaby. When she wasn't looking at him, wasn't trying to control the need to wrap her arms about his neck and kiss him senseless, she could produce some semblance of logical thought. 'We should…uh… probably sit down and change the subject.'

'I can't even think what it is we're supposed to be talking about,' he confessed, which, when Honey opened her eyes to look at him, only made her instincts harder to fight.

'Anything,' she advised. 'Although I am having trouble thinking of a topic.'

'I'm not.' He raised his eyebrows in a suggestive manner before his gaze dipped to her lips. 'I want to kiss you again, Honey. I want to hold you in my arms without the wind and rain blustering around us. I want to feel your body pressed against mine. I want to run my hands through your hair, to press tiny kisses to your soft skin and to press my lips to yours in a way that makes my blood boil over.'

The primordial need in his tone was echoed in his eyes and it caused her to tremble as she never had before. It wasn't that she was scared of him, quite the opposite, in fact. She couldn't believe how powerful his words were, how they made her feel as though she was the most special woman in the world.

'Edward.' She rested her hands over his heart as she shifted to turn closer to him. Automatically, one arm came about her, drawing her close so he could fulfil his desires and *really* kiss her.

'Honey, you're so unexpected. You've burst into my life like a splash of colour over a dark canvas and you've made me question myself, made me focus my thoughts, made me release my tension by yelling into the wind.' He brushed some loose strands of hair back from her face, his fingers caressing her neck. Honey tipped her head to the side, granting him access, and slowly he bent to press a few tantalising, fluttering kisses to her skin.

'Divine,' he murmured. He lifted his head and stared into her face, placing his fingers beneath her chin and rubbing his thumb over her plump lips. Honey gasped at the touch, her eyes wide in wonderment at the way he was making her feel.

'Edward.' His name was a caress from her lips and while he wanted nothing more than to feel and taste the sweet flavours of her mouth, he also wanted to take his time, to memorise every contour of her face, every crease in her neck, every inch of her body. He couldn't fight the way he was drawn to her any more. He could see by the way she was responding ardently to his touch that she was as committed to these feelings as he was. He wasn't alone.

Honey understood him and the realisation filled him with a powerful sense of peace.

He bent his head and kissed the other side of her neck, oh, so gently applying pressure as he tasted her skin, delighted with the way she seemed to melt further into his hold. She wanted him as much as he wanted her and that knowledge shot straight to his heart.

His heart?

Edward straightened, dropping his hand back to his side, and gazed down into her face. Her eyelids were closed, her body open towards him, displaying complete trust. When she opened her eyes, they had a dazed, dreamy look. Edward swallowed over the knowledge that he shouldn't be leading her on.

Yelling at the wind was one thing but he'd done that with Honey's direction. He needed to seek and find his own direction, to discover who he was. It wasn't fair to Honey for him to be wanting her so desperately like this.

'Edward?' When she'd said his name moments before there had been a sense of awe, as though she hadn't been able to believe he was really holding her, really touching her, really desperate to kiss her. Now he could hear the question in her tone, could see the slight confusion beneath her lashes, could feel her concern starting to rise. How had she been able to feel something had changed? She was a woman who seemed to be so in tune with him that she understood, sometimes even before he did, what was going on. Now was no different.

'What's wrong?' she whispered, licking her lips, her gaze still flicking between his eyes and his mouth.

'I want you.' The words were out before he could stop them, confusion creasing his brow.

Her smile was small. 'I know.' She leaned forward and rested her head on his chest, her hands tucked beneath her chin. He wrapped both arms about her but didn't draw her any closer. It was as though he so desperately wanted to hold her but knew he shouldn't.

Drawing in a deep breath, filling her lungs with the scent of him, Honey eased back. Edward instantly loosened his hold on her. She quickly reached out and grasped the back of the chair where her jumper was slowly drying, her legs still not strong enough to support her. The kisses he'd pressed to her neck had wound her so tight, she was still coming back to earth.

'We need to take things slowly,' she remarked as she sat down at the table.

Edward stood where he was for a second and then raked his hand through his hair. It wasn't that taking things slowly was the problem, as far as he could see, it was the fact that his feelings for Honey seemed to be increasing with every passing moment he spent with her.

Thankfully, Bernadette came over to them, carrying a tray of not only drinks but delicious-smelling food as well. 'Here you go,' she said. 'I had the chef whip you both up some banana and caramel pancakes. They're just new on the menu but on a blustery day like today they're just what the doctor ordered.' Bernadette giggled at her own joke and then left them alone, refusing to accept any payment for the food or drinks, telling them that all doctors involved in medical rescues deserved a free meal.

Edward picked up his fork and forced himself to eat something, more to appease Bernadette, lest she think he didn't like the food, rather than because he was hungry. He searched for a topic of conversation and it appeared Honey was doing the same thing.

'So…on top of Kosciuszko, you said you were almost engaged?' She cut up her pancakes as she spoke.

'That's right.'

'Do you mind if I pry and ask what happened?'

Edward slowly drew in a breath before exhaling. 'Amelia and I met at medical school. I was a few years ahead of her and to earn extra money I started tutoring. She needed help.' He took a sip of his hot chocolate. It was strange telling Honey about his past, not because it made him feel uncomfortable but simply because it didn't. Shouldn't he feel odd telling a woman he'd just kissed about his past relationship?

Honey thought about what he'd said up on the mountain and nodded, the pieces falling into place. 'You both wanted the same things out of life, began to plan your life together and then when your parents passed away, she didn't want the instant family.'

'In a nutshell.' He ate a mouthful of pancakes, watching her closely. 'How about you?' he asked after swallowing. 'What happened to you? Why haven't you met the right man?'

'I was in a disastrous relationship about five years ago and since then I've been more concerned with finding the place where I belong. You see, Kennedy is now head of surgery at Brisbane General hospital. We met when I was doing a six-month locum in A and E. We dated. Things became serious. We started looking at properties, houses, schools for our future children, and it looked as though I was finally going to find that elusive home I'd always been looking for.'

'And then?'

'And then things started to change and I mean *change*. At that stage, my hair was a ginger colour with green tips on the ends. Well, now that we were serious, it had to go. He arranged a hair appointment with his mother's hairdresser to 'put my hair back the right way', I believe were his exact words. Kennedy wasn't happy with the way I dressed, so he went and chose my clothes for me. I came home from work late one night and found bags of beautiful designer clothes in my apartment but none of them were my style. None of them were *me*.'

'Sounds as though he was trying to change you, to make you conform to his idea of the perfect surgeon's wife.'

'Exactly.' Honey shook her head as she remembered, the pain surprisingly not as bad as it had once been. 'He also reserved two places for our two future children at the most prestigious boarding school in Sydney, without ever consulting me. I would *never* send my children to boarding school.' Honey stabbed the table forcefully with her finger. 'To send a child away? Never. I've lived the life of a lonely child and I won't allow it for *my* children. I want to give my children a legacy they can be proud of, just as your parents did for you and your brothers. Besides, I don't want to have only two children, I want a whole gaggle of them, and when I pointed this out to Kennedy, he said I was being foolish.'

Honey took a breath and forced herself to calm down, to shake off the annoyance she felt about Kennedy. 'I thought I'd found my home, the place where I belonged, but it turned out I'd found a prison instead. It made me wonder if I'd ever find the place where I really could spend the rest of my life.'

'So you left.'

'So I left,' she agreed with a nod. 'That was about five years ago now.'

'When you were *really* six years old,' he pointed out with a sad smile, wanting to cheer her up a little bit.

'Just a child,' she sighed.

'Did you return to stay with your grandparents or just move jobs?'

Honey nodded. 'I did actually go back to their place in Sydney and spent some time with them. I don't know, sometimes when things don't work out the way you planned, you need to head back to a comfort zone. It helps to regroup, to focus your mind, to put priorities in order.'

'And what about your parents? Have you ever been back to see them?'

Honey nodded. 'I have. Three years after I left, I returned for Woody's eighteenth birthday. He really wanted me there so I went. It was a disaster. My parents were ashamed I was studying medicine, telling me I'd been brainwashed by society, by my grandparents.'

Edward raised his eyebrows in surprise. 'They weren't happy?'

'No. They wanted me to become a vet, to treat the homeless animals, to run a shelter for them. I told you I was always very good with animals, with caring, with nursing poor little birds, especially oil-soaked penguins, back to health. We had a big row and almost ended up ruining Woody's birthday.'

'How did Woody take it?'

Honey smiled at the mention of her brother. 'He forgave me. He said it was worth a try, getting the family together, but it had been a mistake.'

'So you've stayed in touch with your brother?'

'Always. I left my parents, not my brother. I practically raised Woody. There was no way I was breaking off contact with him. He was almost fifteen when I left so I sent him a cellphone and we were able to keep in touch. My parents don't approve of such devices but Woody always had a way of getting around them, of making them see his point of view, and so they let him keep it. We would talk every week—we still do—but rarely about our parents. I just…don't want to know. The hurt, the neglect, the feeling that everything else in the world was more important to them than their own children still runs deep.'

Edward nodded, understanding her hurt. 'Families aren't easy, Honey. Children aren't easy. I've had countless arguments with my siblings on a brotherly level and when I've been acting the parent. You saw how Hamilton and I were tearing into each other but, believe me, I'd do anything for him. He's my brother. I gave up everything I'd always wanted for him and Ben and I don't regret it. Not one bit, but I do wish I hadn't had to do it. Raising children is…hard. Sometimes I have no clue how my parents coped. Five boys! My poor mother, and I remember that the twins and I used to get into all kinds of mischief.'

'You appreciate your mother more, though, right? What she and your father did for you? How they provided for you? They left you with a legacy, one you have held up high and polished until it shines, but doesn't that make you want to continue passing it on to the next generation? To hand down stories of dreams and hopes?'

'Not really.'

Edward's words stunned her for a second. 'Really? You don't want to have children of your own?'

Edward slowly shook his head. 'Not particularly.' He put his fork down. 'I've done my time. I'm not sure exactly what I'm planning to do once Hamilton leaves home but it isn't to settle down and have children of my own.'

Honey blinked once. Twice, wondering why this news seemed to pierce her heart. Was that the reason why he'd been trying to keep her at arm's length? She'd seen the way he'd struggled with his desire to touch her, to hold her, to kiss her, and she'd been wanting him closer all the while, not putting up any resistance of her own.

'But you're such a good father,' she blurted, unable to keep the shock from her tone. 'How can you not want—?' She stopped herself, putting a hand to her mouth. 'No,' she said a moment later. 'That's your decision. I know it can't have been at all easy for you, taking on the guardianship, giving up your own dreams. Taking the weight of the world on your shoulders. It can't have been easy.'

'Just as it wasn't easy for you either.' Edward pointed out. 'You said you practically raised your brother.'

'Yes, but I wasn't alone. My parents were occasionally around.'

'I think that was the thing I wished for the most. To just spend one more day with my parents, to ask them all the questions I never thought to ask them before they passed away.' He swallowed and slowly shook his head.

'They were taken so suddenly. One minute they were called out to help with an emergency and the next, Pete called with the news that…' He paused, his voice thick. Honey felt a lump start to build in her own throat. 'That they were both dead. Gone.' Edward closed his eyes as the memories and the grief started to rise to the surface.

'See?' He asked a moment later, his eyes snapping open. 'This is why I don't like spending too much time by myself, too much time looking inwards, because nothing I say or do will *ever* bring them back.' He swallowed a few times then cleared his throat. 'You have your parents. They're alive, Honey. Nothing, no misunderstanding, no quarrel, no differing view points are worth it. They're not perfect. My parents weren't perfect. No parent is perfect—as I've discovered the hard way—but your parents are alive, Honey, and that's a good thing.'

She nodded and wiped at the tears stinging behind her

eyes. 'You're right, Edward, but I just don't know what to say. How to face them. What do I do? You said before it was as easy as picking up the phone and saying 'hi' but is it? What happens after that?'

He shrugged. 'I don't know and maybe I'm not the person to advise you. I haven't even been able to go back to Charlotte's Pass since the accident. Lorelai has always done any house calls out there. Peter and Bartholomew took Benedict and Hamilton to see the memorial erected there in honour of those who lost their lives that fateful day but…I can't do it.'

Honey stared. 'You've never been back?'

'No.'

She looked down at their cold food, a crazy idea formulating in her mind…a crazy idea that might just help him out. 'What if…?' she said, raising her eyes to meet his.

'No.' He cut her off.

'Hear me out. What if we go to Charlotte's Pass today? We can go together. I'll hold your hand. I'll help you in any way I can.'

Edward was about to say no again but a stirring deep inside stopped him. Breathing out slowly, he met Honey's gaze. 'What if…we *do* go to Charlotte's Pass today? And what if…you call your parents?'

'They don't have a—'

'Someone in that commune they live in has to have a phone. Your brother would surely have a way to contact them,' Edward replied and Honey nodded, her face almost as pale as the clouds outside. 'I'll help you, if you'll help me.' He held out his hand, palm open.

'Deal?'

Honey pondered for a moment, knowing she'd do anything to help him achieve peace of mind. It seemed

Edward was more than willing to do the same for her. She lifted her hand and slid it into his warm one, unable to ignore the exploding heat that shot through her body at the touch.

'Deal.'

# CHAPTER EIGHT

As THEY drove along the road to Charlotte's Pass, Edward still behind the wheel of Honey's car, she wasn't sure what to say. She could tell he was concentrating on the road but the closer they drew to the alpine village, the tighter he seemed to be gripping the steering-wheel.

'Just as well it's summer,' he murmured as he slowed the car and turned off Kosciuszko road, onto the only road which led to Charlotte's Pass. 'During winter, the only way to access this place is via the SkiTube at Perisher.'

Honey nodded as he slowed the car and parked it outside the main hotel. 'I'm glad we decided to come today.' She climbed from the car and came around to the driver's side. Without hesitation, she reached for his hand and was pleased he didn't shy away. 'How are you doing?' she asked, looking intently into his face. It was colder here than it had been at the restaurant but, oddly enough, she didn't feel the chill. She was so focused, so intent on making sure Edward was really OK with this that for some reason the cold didn't matter.

Inwardly, she was still a little stunned at his declaration about not having children, especially when she knew he'd make such a wonderful father. Hamilton was proof of that and she was sure Benedict was equally as wonderful as the rest of his brothers. If Edward really didn't want to traverse the path of becoming a parent, then she knew she should start to disentangle her emotions from him. However, now was most definitely not the time. If she could do this one thing for Edward, if she could help him, be there for him as he took this enormous step towards healing the pain buried deep within his heart, that would be enough. Or so she hoped. 'Eddie?'

'I'm fine.' He looked at her, seeing the encouragement in her eyes. 'It's the right time.'

'All right.' She didn't let go of his hand but turned to look at the town, which was lush and green. 'Where do we go?'

'The little ecumenical chapel.' Edward pointed up the street to where a large triangular-shaped roof could be seen. 'Up the winding path,' he stated. 'In winter, this whole place is a beautiful blanket of white,' he murmured as they headed up the path. When they reached the top, standing outside the chapel, he turned and looked at the village before him. 'I'd forgotten how beautiful this place is.' He turned and smiled at Honey. 'The memorial is inside the chapel. Peter and Bartholomew spoke to the families of the others who died in the avalanche and it was decided to have the memorial indoors so that it wasn't snowed over during the winter months.'

'Sounds lovely.' He was hesitating a bit and Honey gave his hand a reassuring squeeze. 'Would you like to go in alone? Or would you like me to—?'

'Come with me.' It was a statement, not an answer to her question. Honey immediately nodded and took a step towards the door. Edward quickly opened it and together they went in, side by side, hand in hand.

They stood in the entryway where there were two tables by the door with the parish newsletter and several bibles and hymnals. The walls, to their left and right, were covered in beautiful mosaic art. The one on the right showed sunbeams shining down on the village of Charlotte's Pass. The wall on the left also had a sun shining its beams down but on this wall were a lot of white doves, flying upwards towards the sun, seeming to represent a feeling of complete freedom.

Edward stared at the wall with the doves, his grip on Honey's hand tightening. 'Forty-five doves,' he whispered.

As her eyes started to adjust to the dimmer light, Honey could see a tall, slim man walking towards them, his black and white clerical collar showing at his neck beneath his thin wool jumper.

'Edward!' The chaplain reached out his hand and placed it on Edward's shoulder. 'It's wonderful you've come.'

Edward tore his gaze from the wall to look at the chaplain. He opened his mouth to speak but found he couldn't and Honey realised he was too choked up with emotion. She stepped forward and offered her free hand to the chaplain.

'Hello. I'm Honey. I'm the new locum working in Oodnaminaby.' The chaplain dropped his hand from Edward's shoulder and shook Honey's hand warmly. 'I have to say your chapel here is quite lovely. Very relaxing.'

'I'm glad.' The chaplain looked from Honey to Edward, then down at their joined hands, Edward was holding onto her so tightly she thought she might lose all blood flow fairly soon. She didn't mind. 'I'll give you some privacy.'

Once he'd left, Edward sniffed and took a few steps forward towards the wall with the doves. As they drew closer, Honey realised each dove had a first name painted on it and a lump lodged in her own throat. Her gaze quickly sought out the ones named Hannah and Cameron and a moment later Edward reached out his free hand and touched each of them with trembling fingers.

He sniffed again and she leaned into him, putting her arm about his waist, drawing him closer. A tear slid down his cheek and he nodded slowly before pulling her close. It was as though he needed the warmth of her live body, to reassure himself that life did go on.

'It's…uh…beautiful.' He wrapped both arms about her and rested his chin on her head. 'I know they're gone. I've known for a long time but…um…this…' He sniffed again and she could hear the choked emotion in his tone. 'This makes it…more real.' He held his breath for a moment before sucking air into his lungs. 'They're gone, Honey, and I loved them so much.'

Honey couldn't hold back her own tears any longer and allowed them to flow silently down her cheeks. When she sniffed, Edward leaned back and looked down into her face, seeing how touched she was by the death of people she'd never met.

'I'm proud of you,' she whispered.

'Thank you,' he said, and bent to brush his lips lightly over hers, his voice filled with emotional relief. 'Thank you.'

The end of Honey's second week at Oodnaminaby wasn't as exciting as the first but that didn't bother her. They'd received word from Cooma hospital that Leonard was progressing well after undergoing orthopaedic surgery to stabilise his right leg and arm, as well as receiving sutures to the gash on the back of his head. It was hoped he'd make a full recovery in time.

At the clinic, her patient lists had settled down now that everyone had come and met the new doctor in town. Even when she was out and about in town or surround-

ing districts, doing house calls or just seeing the country-
side, Honey was always greeted with a cheery smile and
a wave. It also meant that Lorelai could stay at home full
time and off her feet.

The baby's head was now completely engaged and even
though Lorelai was only thirty-six weeks, it was clear she
could deliver at any time. Honey had arranged a briefing
with Edward to ensure she knew the protocols for trans-
ferring Lorelai to Tumut hospital, should that become necessary.

Since their trip to Mt Kosciuszko and then to Charlotte's
Pass, Honey had found Edward to be a little embarrassed
around her. There was no disputing the fact they had feelings for each other but after the emotional moments they'd
shared in the small chapel, Edward had been keeping his
distance.

Professionally, they discussed their patients and went
about business as usual. Twice during the week he'd invited her to share dinner with himself and Hamilton and
on each occasion he hadn't made any move to touch her.
He was polite and charming and obviously as confused
about his emotions as she was.

With Edward declaring he didn't want to have children,
Honey had started to figure out what meant more to her.
Was it finding a place to call home or finding a place to
raise her children? She'd always thought they'd be the
same place but now she wasn't so sure. It was true that
she'd fallen in love with Ood, not only with the breath-
taking scenery but also with the people of the community.
It was definitely a place she could call home and it was
definitely a great place to raise a family but with the way
her feelings for Edward were refusing to be quashed, she
wasn't sure she'd be able to stay on past her twelve-month
contract. Confusion continued to reign and she found

concentrating on work was the best thing she could do right now.

'I'm so used to being busy,' Lorelai said as the two women caught up for a soothing cup of herbal tea. 'I've always been at the surgery, doing house calls in the district or visiting patients in Tumut or Cooma hospitals. Now I'm home all the time, I keep startling John.' Lorelai sipped her tea as Honey massaged her feet, using the pressure points to relieve the tension in the pregnant woman's back. 'Do you know, he walked into the room the other day, talking on the phone, and almost jumped through the ceiling when he realised I was lying on the lounge with my feet up, reading a book.'

Honey was surprised to hear Lorelai's husband was so jumpy. 'I thought John worked for the mining company as a demolition expert,' she remarked. 'I wouldn't have thought that was the type of profession to lend itself to a jumpy worker.'

'You'd think that,' Lorelai agreed. 'He says he has to be so alert and focused at work that at home he tends to let all his control go.'

'Hmm.' Honey heard something else in Lorelai's tone, something she couldn't quite put her finger on. 'How did the two of you meet?'

'On the ski-slopes. John's always been an avid skier.' Lorelai smiled, reflecting back on the past. 'We started dating almost straight away and before the next ski season we were married and he'd moved in here with me.'

'You didn't buy the house together?'

'No. I bought the house outright when I came back to Ood to practise medicine.' Lorelai frowned and sipped her tea. 'Thank goodness it's still in my name.'

Honey was surprised at her words. 'Is everything all right with you and John?'

Lorelai's eyes instantly teared up and Honey quickly took the cup away lest she spilled the hot liquid and passed her a tissue. 'I don't know what's going on, Honey. He's snappy at me all the time. He says I'm fat.'

'You're pregnant,' Honey remarked, kneeling by her friend and putting her arms around her, anger building towards Lorelai's husband. She'd only met him once and her first impression had not been at all positive. John had leered at Honey's body, his lips smirking as though he thought she was a fruitcake because of the way she dressed, and then with a blink of his eyes he'd dismissed her. It had made her wonder what had attracted Lorelai to him in the first place.

'He wasn't like that when we met,' Lorelai said be-tween sobs, and for a second Honey thought she'd mused out loud. 'He was attentive and sweet and kind. He was happy to live here in Oodnaminaby, to get a job in the district and to ski all winter long. He'd often stay up at the lodge in Thredbo, helping his friends who worked there pack up and set up each day. Sometimes the roads were too slushy to drive on, or he'd lend his tyre chains to someone else, which meant he couldn't drive home...' Lorelai trailed off as though all the excuses sounded too convenient.

'He didn't want to have the baby,' she confessed to Honey in a tiny whisper. 'I haven't told anyone that. Not my dad, not Edward or any of the boys.' She hiccuped, her bottom lip wobbling. 'When I told him I was pregnant, he told me to get a termination and then went to the pub.'

'Oh, Lore.' Honey's hatred for the man intensified. 'I had no idea.'

'No one does...and I've been able to keep my own mind under control while I was working but now that I'm home all the time, I keep going over and over things, my mind churning, and…' A fresh bout of tears erupted. 'And then I can't stop crying,' she blubbed.

Honey held her friend, passed her tissues and allowed Lorelai to let go of all the angst, pain and devastation she'd obviously been holding onto for far too long.

'Thank you,' Lorelai said, after blowing her nose again. 'I think I needed to get that out.'

'Another cup of tea?' Honey asked, but Lorelai yawned.

'No, thanks. I think I'll have a snooze.'

'Here on the couch? Or do you want to lie down in your bed?'

'Here's fine.'

'OK. Let's get you comfortable and I'll give your back a rub.' Honey shifted some cushions until Lorelai was comfortable and settled, then began a low back massage.

'Thanks for listening,' Lorelai remarked.

'That's what friends are for.'

As Honey continued to massage, her thoughts naturally drifted to Edward. Every day when she saw him at the clinic, her heart would leap and her body would warm with memories of his arms about her, his breath mingling with hers, his mouth pressing those soft, sweet butterfly kisses to her skin, heating her body until she thought she might explode. She thought of the way he'd held her when they'd been in that small chapel in Charlotte's Pass, about the way he'd kissed her and said thank you. Her heart started to ache for him, for the pain he must have felt seeing that beautiful memorial to his parents and the other people who had lost their lives in the avalanche.

After they'd left the chapel, she'd accepted the car keys and driven them safely back to Ood, letting Edward know how courageous he'd been and how much she admired him. As she continued to rub Lorelai's back gently, the pregnant woman dozing, Honey realised her feelings for Edward were intensifying with each passing day.

On Sunday evening, Honey had decided on an early night and was dressed in her tie-dyed pyjama bottoms and a matching snug singlet top. She'd made the garments a few years ago when she'd been working in Queensland and the weather had been particularly hot and humid. It wasn't particularly hot now but the garments gave her a sense of comfort, a sense of being herself.

When the phone rang, Honey rushed to pick it up, hoping, longing for it to be Edward. 'I've cooked too much food for dinner,' he would say, in that deep hypnotic voice of his. 'Why don't you come and join us?' At least, that's how it played out in her fantasy world.

'Hello? Honey speaking,' she said.

'Yo, sis.' Woody's deep voice came down the line.

'Yo, bro,' she replied in her usual way, but couldn't keep the slight hint of disappointment out of her voice. She leaned over to the kitchen window and twitched back the lace curtain, looking out to where she could just see the back of the main house, hoping for a glimpse of Edward, but she was out of luck.

'Expecting someone else to call?' Woody asked.

'What?' Honey returned her attention to her brother. 'Sorry. No. Uh…how's things? Recovering from your last trip to Tarparnii? How's Nilly and the girls?'

Woody laughed. 'They're fine. What about you? How are things going? Still being asked out to dinner every night? We didn't get much of a chance to talk last week you were such hot property.'

Honey sighed and curled up on a chair, closing her eyes. 'Things have settled down a bit.' Except for her heartbeat every time she looked at Edward. She shook her head, trying to clear her thoughts and concentrate on her conversation with her brother. 'The town is nice, the people are…' She paused. '*Very* welcoming.'

'Aha. I knew it. You've met a man.'

'What? How can you possibly tell that from—?'

'I know you, sis.' Woody's chuckle came down the phone line and she knew it was futile to try and kid him. 'Looks as though I'm going to have to come to town for a visit and check him out.'

Her eyes snapped open. 'Don't you dare.'

'In fact, that's not a bad idea. I was thinking of coming and catching up with you in person for a change. I'll be heading to see Mum and Dad next week and Oodnaminaby isn't too far from where they're situated at the moment so I can just pop on down, meet this bloke who's caught your eye, ask him if his intentions are honourable and slide on outta town, back to my own life.'

'I always love to see you, Woody, you know that.' Honey paused, remembering the deal she'd struck with Edward, the one where he would face his past if she faced hers. She swallowed and cleared her throat, knowing she had to follow through on that promise. The thought of letting Edward down was something she couldn't do. 'Uh… you said Mum and Dad were close by?'

'Yeah. They're in Victoria at the moment, at La Trobe Valley. About a day's drive from where you are.'

'Oh. That *is* close.' Closer than they'd been to each other in a very long time. She swallowed over the dryness in her throat but forced herself to go on. She'd promised Edward. 'Do you have a contact for them? A phone number of someone in their commune or—'

'They have a phone, Hon.'

She frowned. 'A cellphone?'

'Yeah. That way they can stay in touch with me whenever I'm in Tarparnii.'

'Oh. I never thought they'd ever—'

'A lot has changed, Hon. *They've* changed. So have you. It'd make me happy to have my family back together again. Have you got a pen? I'll give you the number.'

Honey took down the number and chatted with her brother for a few more minutes before a beep sounded, indicating she had another call coming through. 'Sorry, Woody. I have to go. I'll talk to you soon and...uh... thanks, bro. Love you oodles.' Honey disconnected the call and then pressed the button to connect her new call. 'Honey speaking,' she said.

'Honey?' It was Lorelai and she sounded incredibly upset.

'Lore? What's wrong? Are you feeling all right? Any contractions?'

'Everything's wrong,' Lorelai answered, bursting into tears over the phone. 'John's having an affair,' she mumbled between sobs. 'He just came right out and told me.'

'I'm on my way.' Honey wasn't a hundred per cent surprised at this news and quickly found a pair of flip-flops, sliding her feet into them, her cellphone still held to her ear. 'Keep talking to me, Lorelai. Tell me everything.'

She collected a torch and then headed outside, a brisk March wind instantly cooling her skin. She should have picked up a cardigan but it didn't matter. Lorelai was all that mattered. Her friend continued to sob and talk down the line with Honey only managing to understand about every third word, but it was when Lorelai groaned in pain, a deep guttural sound, that Honey stopped walking. She was in the driveway at the front of Edward's house.

'What was that?' she asked, and heard Lorelai almost panting. 'Was that a push?' When Lorelai gasped for breath and made another grunting sound, Honey raced up the front steps of Edward's house and rang the door-bell, trying desperately to curb her impatience to ring twice when he didn't answer immediately.

'Hold on. I'm just getting Eddie,' she told Lorelai as the front door opened. There he stood. The man she was hard pressed to stop thinking about, dressed once more in a pair of old denims and nothing else. His hair was damp from his shower and she wondered whether his delay in opening the door was because he'd just finished.

She breathed in, opening her mouth to tell him about Lorelai, but his fresh, spicy scent curled its way around her, teasing her, enticing her. She closed her mouth and swallowed as her gaze roved over the incredible contours of his chest.

'Honey?' Lorelai's upset voice came down the phone, which Honey still held to her ear. Honey blinked and quickly looked away from the sexy man before her. How was she supposed to fight the way he made her feel when he dressed like that and only created even more fantasies for her to think about?

'Honey?' Edward opened the screen door, his gaze rov-ing over her body just as hers had over his. He sucked in a breath, wishing she'd had the sense to put more on be-fore ringing his doorbell, especially at this time of night, when his thoughts had already been on her.

The tie-dyed hippy look suited her, especially when her long, silky hair was flowing loosely around her shoulders. The pants she wore were baggy enough but the top... He swallowed over the lump that came to his throat at the way the tight-fitting top highlighted her figure. She looked so incredibly sexy and he clenched his jaw, knowing he needed to fight the mounting attraction that existed be-tween them.

'You could have used the back d—' It was then he re-alised she was talking to someone on the phone and that there was a crinkle furrowing her otherwise perfect brow. 'Honey? What's wrong?'

She lifted her gaze to meet his, trying desperately hard to ignore his manly chest in the process. 'It's Lorelai. She's in labour.'

Panic momentarily flitted across his face before he clenched his jaw and nodded. 'Right. Let me get my bag.' He disappeared for fifteen seconds and came back with his medical bag in hand. 'I've had it packed ready for a delivery as I had a hunch Lore wasn't going to make it to the hospital in time to have the baby,' he said as they walked, Honey still talking to their friend on the phone. She was thankful, though, that Edward had donned a shirt, cover-ing up the skin her fingers were still itching to touch.

When they arrived at Lorelai's home a little later, they were met by a pacing, sobbing woman. She disconnected the phone and threw it down onto the lounge cushions be-fore wiping furiously at the tears which were blurring her vision.

'I'm so glad you're both here,' she said between her tears. 'At least someone still loves me.'

'Oh, Lorelai.' Honey put her arms around her friend, providing much-needed reassurance. 'Let's get you sorted out,' she said as they walked further into the house. 'Have you had many contractions or just the really big one on the phone?'

'A few twinges. It's all been much the same for the past few days,' Lorelai answered, the usually calm and con-trolled woman completely flustered. 'I just thought they were more intense Braxton-Hicks contractions.'

'You've been under a lot of pressure, Lorelai,' Honey

soothed. 'However, both Eddie and I are here and we're going to take excellent care of you.'

Edward put his hands on Lorelai's shoulders to stop her from pacing. 'You're in a right state, Lore. Let's get you to the bedroom where you can lie down and Honey can examine you.'

'No!' Lorelai spun away from him and resumed her pacing. 'No way. I'm not going into *that* bedroom ever again.'

'Why?' Edward looked from one woman to the other, his brow creased in total confusion.

'You didn't tell him!' Lorelai looked at Honey.

'I was talking to you on the phone the entire way here,' Honey remarked, keeping her voice nice and calm, cool and soothing. The fact that Lorelai was too caught up in the emotion of her husband's infidelities was starting to affect the baby. 'Sit down, Lorelai. I need to take your blood pressure,' she murmured as she opened Edward's emergency bag and pulled out the portable sphygmomanometer.

Edward ushered her to one of the comfortable armchairs. They were all quiet while Honey took the blood-pressure reading. 'Just as I'd suspected. Rising. We need to calm you down, sweetie.' Now that Lorelai was sitting, Honey quickly removed the woman's slip-on shoes and applied pressure to the base of her big toe.

'*He* didn't do this,' Lorelai murmured after a moment, rubbing a hand over her swollen abdomen, her tension starting to flow away under Honey's care.

'Who?' Edward asked.

'John. I told him exactly where to press and told him it would relieve the pressure and pain I was getting but he didn't do it. He didn't care about me, or about our baby.'

'What did he say?' Honey asked, trying to keep herself

calm yet internally she was completely riled up against the insensitive jerk Lorelai had married.

'What did who say?' Edward asked, completely perplexed as he plugged in the portable foetal heart monitor he'd extracted from his bag.

'John's having an affair.' Lorelai blurted the words out.

'*What?*' Edward went from complete and utter astonishment to a deep, angry scowl in a matter of seconds. 'Where is he?'

'He's gone. I confronted him tonight and he didn't deny it. Told me outright he'd been having an affair for the last eight months. *Eight months!* Then he said he was glad I knew. That he was relieved he no longer had to lie to me or to sneak around or to pretend to be interested in me and the baby.' Lorelai slumped further into the comfy chair, her expression filled with hurt and disbelief.

'He said I was always working and that I was more interested in my patients than in him.' Lorelai looked at Edward. 'Is that true? Am I?'

'No, Lore. This isn't your fault. His infidelities are not *your* fault. They're his. He's weak-willed and spineless. You're a kind, caring woman who is now in labour.' He glanced at Honey, as though seeking confirmation, and received a nod as the answer. 'Let's focus on bringing this baby into the world. That's what's important right now.' He clenched his jaw. He and his brothers would see to John later. No one hurt *his* surrogate sister and simply walked away without facing the consequences.

'Eddie's right. Listen to this.' Honey placed the microphone of the foetal heart monitor onto Lorelai's abdomen. The three adults were silent, the only sound filling the air was one of a fast but healthy heartbeat. 'Perfect,' Honey remarked after reading the display from the machine. 'Now, where do you want to have the baby?'

'At Tumut hospital,' Lorelai said, but Honey shook her head.

'Sorry, love. You pushed once while I was on the phone to you. That means we're not going anywhere, otherwise we risk you delivering in an ambulance. Better to keep you here, nice and comfortable. If you don't want to go and lie down on your bed, then what would you like? What's going to feel the most comfortable for you? Beanbag? Floor? Squatting?'

'Beanbag,' Lorelai remarked after a moment, then her lower lip quivered again as fresh tears sprang to her eyes. 'I can't believe he's gone. He was supposed to be here with me, watching our baby being born, but he told me tonight he doesn't want me and he doesn't want the b-b-baby.' Tears bubbled over but a moment later Lorelai was racked with another contraction.

Edward met Honey's gaze over Lorelai's head. His expression said they needed to get Lorelai settled and to focus on preparing for this birth. Honey nodded in agreement, not a single spoken word passing between them.

They worked together to get Lorelai into position, Edward going to the linen cupboard to gather some clean sheets and towels and to prepare an area to receive the baby once it was born.

'You *have* done this before?' he quickly confirmed as Lorelai rested between contractions, which had now escalated to a firm five minutes apart. Concern and worry peppered Edward's brow and Honey rubbed her hand up and down his arm, wanting to reassure him, especially as Lorelai was the closest thing he had to a sister.

'Yes, Eddie, I have. In fact, I've delivered twenty-eight babies. This one will be number twenty-nine and only two of those were in a hospital. All the others were home births. Lorelai is almost fully dilated and at this stage the delivery looks as though it's going to be textbook. You've packed the medical bag with everything I need, the Tumut paramedics are on standby, so we're good to go.' She nodded for emphasis, then turned and looked at their friend, sliding her hand down to his arm to squeeze his fingers. 'Lorelai and the baby will be just fine.'

'Medically speaking or emotionally speaking?' Edward asked softly, so Lorelai couldn't hear them. Honey could hear the anger and disgust at John in his tone.

'She has good support. *That* makes an enormous difference.' Lorelai's breathing started to increase. 'Ahh... next contraction on the way. That's our cue,' she remarked, and they both shifted back into position.

Over the next four hours Honey and Edward supported Lorelai, who was doing all the hard work. She listened to Honey's instructions about when to push and when not to push. Edward acted as support for Lorelai, sponging her down and keeping her cool and as comfortable as possible, as well as ensuring Honey had everything she required.

At twenty-eight minutes past two in the morning, Honey finished delivering the beautiful baby girl. Edward did the honours and cut the cord, before accepting the baby from Honey to wrap up and perform an Apgar test.

Lorelai had collapsed back onto the beanbag, not having the energy to care about any thing. Honey delivered the placenta and checked it carefully, pleased with the result. Meanwhile, little healthy cries filled the air as the baby made herself known.

'Sounds as though she doesn't like being poked and prodded.' Honey laughed, watching as Edward expertly wrapped the baby and held her like a loving uncle. She swallowed over the sudden lump in her throat at the sight he made. Man with babe. So gorgeous. So precious. So... right.

'What's the verdict?' Honey asked as she placed the placenta into a disposable container so it could be more thoroughly analysed at a later date. She continued to tidy things up and pulled off the gloves and apron she'd used to protect her clothes.

'One minute Apgar was a seven. Five minutes is a nine. She is strong and healthy and incredibly gorgeous. Lore? Do you want to hold her?'

A very weary Lorelai opened her arms, her eyes still closed, but the moment Edward handed her the baby Lorelai opened her eyes and looked at her daughter. Edward stood next to Honey and both of them watched as in that one instant Lorelai fell in love with her baby girl.

Tears filled Honey's eyes and she slipped her arms around Edward's waist, pleased when he didn't push her away but instead drew her closer, resting his arm on her shoulders.

'What are you going to call her?' Edward asked, his voice thick with emotion.

Lorelai smiled but shook her head. 'I don't know. The names John and I chose no longer seem appropriate. Any suggestions?' she asked, unable to tear her gaze away from her darling cherub.

Honey laughed. 'Don't ask me. My name's so overly hyphenated it's not funny.'

'I think your name is the prettiest name I've ever heard,' Edward remarked softly. 'Honeysuckle Lilly-Pilly Huntington-Smythe.' He looked down at her and exhaled slowly. 'It suits you.'

Honey's throat went dry at the expression she saw in his eyes. It was of complete surrender as though in that one moment in time nothing else in the world mattered except for the two of them. Somehow Edward had the ability to make her feel more special, more precious, more feminine than anyone else she'd ever met. There it was again, the meeting of their two hearts, intertwining, drawing them together.

'Can you two stop making eyes at each other for a few minutes and help me to choose an equally lovely name for my baby girl?'

Lorelai's words startled Edward and he immediately shifted back, a little self-conscious at being caught. Honey knelt down beside her friend. 'Let me look at this cherub,' she said, and brushed the back of her finger over the baby's cheek. 'Oh, she *is* beautiful, Lorelai. So perfectly made.'

'She is. She's *my* baby girl. Mine and only mine.' Her voice choked on the last word but she shook her head, pushing the negative emotions aside. 'Happy thoughts. This is a happy moment. Honey, what's your mother's name?'

'Star.'

Edward looked at her. 'Seriously?'

'Yep. What about your mother's name, Eddie? That's a pretty name,' Honey pointed out. 'I love that seat in the garden, the one dedicated to your parents.'

Edward nodded. 'Hannah.' He and Lorelai spoke at the same time.

'I always admired your mother so much, Edward. She was always there for me.' Lorelai looked down at her baby girl. 'Hannah.'

'Hannah means graceful and pure,' Honey remarked. 'What was your mother's name, Lore?'

'Emily.'

'That means honest and caring.'

'How do you know these things?' Edward shook his head in bemusement. 'You're like a walking name-meaning encyclopedia.'

'I've always found names interesting. Edward, for instance, means guard or rich guard, and you are certainly that. Guarding your family, keeping those who mean the most to you safe.' Honey smiled at him. 'It suits you.'

Lorelai sighed with happiness. 'That's it, then. She's definitely going to be Hannah Emily. That's my girl.' Lorelai kissed Hannah's forehead and the baby snuggled into her mother as though completely exhausted from being born.

'It's a perfect name,' Honey said.

'A perfect name for a perfectly made little girl,' Edward agreed. They were all quiet, absorbed in the tranquillity of the moment, before Lorelai turned sharply to look at her friends, her gaze narrowing on Honey.

'Sorry, but did I hear you call him *Eddie*?'

Honey smiled and nodded at her friend. 'I see your logical thought processes are kicking back into gear, and speaking of getting back into gear, let's get this place cleaned up so you and the lovely Hannah can get comfortable.'

Soon Lorelai was reclining on the couch, her baby still wrapped and in her arms. 'Isn't she going to want a feed? Shouldn't she be hungry? All the books say they're usually hungry when they're born.'

Honey shook her head. 'Sometimes they are and it appears Hannah isn't. Books tend to generalise too much. Don't you worry. Hannah will let you know when she's hungry and I'll be here to help you out.'

'You're a lactation specialist as well?' This question came from Edward, who was on the phone to Tumut hospital, informing them of the uneventful birth of Hannah Emily. 'Is there anything you can't do, Honey?'

'No,' she said with a smile. 'But again I've had a lot of practice with home births. There's no stress, no tension here, Lorelai. You can do whatever you need to do and relax whilst doing it. We can get a bath ready for Hannah and you can freshen up and have a shower. If you're hungry or thirsty, I can fix you something. There's absolutely no pressure.'

Lorelai took in a deep breath, letting it out slowly, and dropped a kiss to her daughter's sleeping head. 'No pressure,' she sighed, and looked at her friend. 'What I really want to know is…' she glanced over at Edward and then back at Honey '…what's going on with you two?'

'I don't know, Lore.' Honey looked over to where Edward was talking on the phone, her heart hammering against her chest with delight.

'But you were hugging him.'

Honey's smile was instant. 'We'd just witnessed the miracle of birth and, well…at that moment it felt right to hug him.'

'I think there's more going on between the two of you than either of you is admitting.'

'What makes you say that?'

'You keep calling him Eddie. *No one* but his mother ever called him Eddie and even then it was more a term of endearment than a common occurrence.'

'He hasn't asked me to stop.'

'That alone speaks volumes,' Lorelai pointed out.

'Besides, I think it suits him.' She thought of the way he'd stood on top of the mountain and yelled ridiculous things into the wind, a smile touching her lips. He was a fine man, an honourable man and an incredibly sexy one at that. Thinking of him opening the door tonight, wearing only jeans, made her mouth go dry.

'I also heard that the two of you went to Charlotte's Pass last weekend.'

Honey was surprised. 'How did you know?'

Lorelai shook her head. 'Honey, Honey, Honey. This part of the country is small and word tends to get around. I don't know how you managed to get him there but I am so glad you did. So are his brothers, but it does stand to reason that only a very special woman, one he lets call him Eddie, would have been able to persuade him to go. You obviously mean a lot to him.'

Honey glanced again at Edward, and when he looked across the room and caught her staring at him, she didn't look away. Instead she smiled and a moment later he returned that smile then gave his attention to whoever he was talking to on the phone.

Hannah started to murmur and squeak and wriggle. 'Looks as though she might be getting ready for a bath.' Honey rubbed her finger over Hannah's little cheek. 'It's exhausting work, being born. Isn't it, missy?'

Honey went and prepared the baby bath, pleased Lorelai was so well set up. Edward came over and watched as Lorelai expertly held her daughter, bathing her so carefully, so gently, so lovingly. Hannah relaxed, quite content, her eyes still closed tight as she allowed herself to float in the warm water.

'It looks as though Miss Hannah likes her bath,' Edward remarked, smiling down at the baby. He'd been watching the way Honey controlled the entire situation where Lorelai was concerned. The whole birth and the aftermath had flowed like a well-orchestrated ballet and he knew it was all Honey's doing. Given what Lorelai had discovered tonight, the fact that her husband's infidelity and the way he rejected her and walked out had caused her to go into labour, the whole situation could have been fraught with out-of-control emotions. Instead, Honey had kept Lorelai focused, had spoken calmly to her, reassured her every step of the way, making sure Lorelai and Hannah moved at their own pace.

Seeing her so in command, not flustered, not concerned, had only raised his opinion of her even more. She was an amazingly skilled woman and he knew how fortunate they were to have her at the Oodnaminaby practice.

He closed his eyes for a second as memories washed over him. Holding her in his arms, up on the mountain, their plastic ponchos blowing in the wind. Being close to her and brushing his lips across her long, smooth neck when they'd been in the restaurant. Feeling the reassurance from the little squeeze she'd given his hand when they'd been in the chapel. Having her close as he'd opened his past and grieved for his parents. All in all, Honeysuckle was becoming incredibly difficult to resist.

'Here, Uncle Edward.' At Honey's sweet voice, he opened his eyes and looked directly into hers as she handed him a towel. 'Get ready to receive the baby and hold your new niece.'

Edward took the towel from her, their hands touching for an instant, awareness flaring between them. 'Wait.' He held her hand through the towel. 'You don't have your contacts in,' he murmured.

'No. Didn't have time to put them in so don't go asking me to read things that are far away.'

He looked deeply at her. 'Wow. Your eyes are…the colour of the sea on a stormy day. Vibrant blue and deep green, mixed together with a hint of grey.' He swallowed. 'Mesmerising.'

'Oh, Eddie, you do pick the strangest times to say and do the sweetest things.' Honey moved out of the way as Lorelai finished bathing Hannah and lifted her out, Edward more than happy to accept the newest addition to Oodnaminaby. He cradled her sweetly in his arms and brushed a kiss on her forehead.

'I'll go find her some clothes to wear,' Lorelai said, as she walked slowly up the corridor towards the nursery, leaving Honey alone with Edward, watching him hold the beautiful baby lovingly in his arms.

'You're good at that,' Honey remarked, her heart tightening at the sight of man and babe together.

'Holding babies? I've had plenty of practice. I was fifteen by the time Hamilton was born and as such was expected to pitch in wherever necessary.'

Honey stepped close and brushed her fingers over Hannah's forehead and cheeks. 'I know you said you didn't want children but look at you. You're a natural. You'd make such a wonderful father,' she said softly.

'That may be so but a family of my own isn't on my agenda at this point.'

Honey nodded and leaned forward to touch little Hannah's hand. She felt as though Edward had just put her in her place and that place was at arm's length from where he stood.

In less than twelve months she'd probably be getting ready to move from Oodnaminaby to… She sighed and clenched her teeth, unable to finish the thought. She didn't want to go from Ood. Of that much she was certain but could she stay in town, living near Edward, seeing him every day, when her feelings for him seemed to be sky-rocketing with each passing moment?

# CHAPTER NINE

Two nights after the birth Honey was just sitting down to a bowl of soup and a piece of toast when there was knock at the coach-house door. Rising, she quickly went to open it and found Hamilton standing there, in his sports gear, dirt smudged on his face.

'Hi,' he said.

'Hi,' she returned brightly. 'Something wrong?'

'Uh…not really.' Hamilton looked past her and pointed to the food on the table. 'You've already eaten?'

'Just about to.'

'Well…uh…' Hamilton shifted from foot to foot.

Honey fixed him with a glare. 'What's wrong?'

'Come for dinner.'

'Did Edward send you over to ask?'

'No, but come anyway.'

'Hamilton.' There was a warning tone in her voice.

'OK, look. I might have done something a little crazy at school today and he's going to find out about it and I thought if you were there for dinner, then you'd be able to keep him all calm and relaxed like you usually do. He's different around you, Honey. He's…like a normal human being. You know…happy!'

Honey couldn't help but laugh. 'How's he going to find out about this thing that happened at school?'

'I have a note to give him.'

'Were you in the wrong? Did you do the wrong thing?'

Hamilton pondered this for a moment. 'Possibly.'

'Ahh.' Honey reached for her long cardigan, which was by the door, and slipped her feet into a pair of leather sandals. 'Then, before you give him the note, explain your side of the story, tell him what happened and whatever the punishment—do not dispute it. You keep saying you want Edward to treat you like a grown-up—that means you start taking the consequences for your actions. If you s*how* him you *are* an adult, he'll treat you like one.'

'Promise?'

'Promise.' She flicked off the lights and headed over with him to the house. 'Surprise,' she said when they both walked into the kitchen. Edward was just taking a dish from the oven. 'Hamilton invited me over for dinner. I hope you don't mind.'

Edward looked from his brother to the woman he couldn't stop thinking about. 'Uh…no.'

'Great. Knew it would be all right,' the teenager said. 'OK. I'm off to have a shower.'

'A quick one,' Edward called as Hamilton raced from the room. Honey was a little startled to find herself alone with Edward. Did Hamilton have another agenda as well? One that included giving the two of them a little push? 'How was clinic today?' he asked as he stirred whatever was in the crockery pot. 'I didn't get to catch up with you before I left.'

'It was good. No surprises. You?'

'Same.'

She walked closer and leaned over the bench, breathing in the delicious aroma of whatever he was making. 'Smells good.'

'So do you,' he murmured, unable to control his words.

He put down the tea-towel he was holding and reached for her hand, drawing her closer. 'I'm glad Hamilton asked you over because I was going to but I didn't want to bother you. I haven't been able to get you off my mind and...' He pressed his mouth to hers, effectively ending whatever it was he'd been saying.

Honey wasn't about to quibble and lifted her head, eager for the touch of his mouth against hers, eager to match his impatient hunger, eager to show him just how much she loved him.

'Good heavens, Honey.' He broke off a moment later, his breathing heavy as his arms came about her waist, needing her even closer. 'I can't stop thinking about you.'

'I know the feeling.'

'I keep wanting to contrive reasons for seeing you, for spending time with you, for being near.'

She smiled against his mouth. 'There's no need to contrive, Edward. I'm open to your suggestions and, in fact, I was actually going to pop over after dinner to ask for your help.'

'Really?' He kissed her cheeks, first one, then the other. 'What do you need help with? Kissing? Because I'm all ready to practise that with you.' To show her he meant what he said, he brought his mouth to hers again, capturing her lips with his, drawing forth a response that left her light-headed and very weak at the knees.

'What is this thing between us?' he murmured.

*Love?*

The word was on the tip of her tongue but she simply didn't have the courage to voice it. What if she said it and he pushed her away? She wasn't sure she was strong enough to deal with that. He kissed her again before eventually drawing back and putting a bit of distance between them.

'You're too distracting. Go and sit at the table or stand

on the other side of the room because otherwise we risk the dinner being burnt or, worse, Hamilton catching us kissing in the kitchen.'

'Uh…I think he already knows.' Honey collected another place setting from the drawer and walked to the table.

'What?'

'He has some bad news to break to you and he wanted me here for moral support. He said I relaxed you, that you were happier when I was around. He's not a kid any more, Eddie.'

'So I'm beginning to realise.' He turned back to the dinner, putting the crockery pot back into the oven. 'So?' he asked a moment later, turning to look at her from the other side of the room. 'What did you need my help with?'

'I uh…spoke to my brother the other night. The night Lore went into labour, actually, so it's been a little busy since then but…uh…he…Woody gave me my parents' phone number.' She shrugged. 'Apparently, they have a cellphone now.'

Edward nodded. 'You're ready to call them?'

'No.' She laughed without humour and shook her head. 'I'm far too scared to call them. That's why I need your help. What am I supposed to say?'

'Hi. How are you? What have you been up to for the past decade? Would you like to come to town for a visit?'

'Visit?'

Edward wiped his hands on the tea-towel, then tossed it aside, closing the distance between them. He placed his hands on her shoulders and looked into her eyes. 'You're a strong woman, Honey. You're supportive, you're kind, you're caring. You can do this. You can reach out to them. You can bridge this vast chasm that divides the three of you.'

Honey nodded, unable to believe how calm he made her feel. With Edward by her side she had the feeling she could accomplish anything. If he believed in her, she could believe in herself.

'I can put dinner on hold and we can call them right now, if you like.'

'Now?'

He nodded and returned to the oven, turning down the temperature before crossing to the phone on the wall. He took it from its cradle and carried it to her. 'Do you have the number?'

She tapped the side of her head. 'I've read it over and over so many times since Woody gave it to me that I've memorised it.'

'Go ahead. Make that call.' He steered her to the table and sat down beside her. Honey simply stared at the phone, paralysed with fear.

'What if they hang up when they hear my voice?' she asked.

Edward shook his head. 'Not going to happen.' He took the phone from her slim fingers. 'What's the number?'

Honey took a deep breath and looked at Edward. She thought about the way he'd looked at her when they'd been standing in that chapel and she remembered how brave he'd been and how proud she'd felt. Now it was her turn. Edward had lost his parents and would never see them again. She had the opportunity and the time to right past wrongs.

'You can do it,' he said, and leaned over to give her an encouraging kiss. Honey swallowed and cleared her throat before closing her eyes and breathing out slowly. Edward believed in her. That was enough.

Opening her eyes, she pressed the connect button. As the ringing tone sounded in her ear, she bit her lip, desperate to control her breathing. A moment later the call connected.

'Hello?' It was her mother's voice and at the sound Honey became paralysed with fear. 'Hello?'

'Go on,' Edward whispered and nodded, a smile on his gorgeous mouth.

Honey swallowed again. 'Mum?'

Her mother breathed in a sharp breath. 'Honeysuckle?' she whispered. 'Is that really you?'

'Yes, it is. Mum…' Emotion choked her throat.

'Oh, Honeysuckle,' her mother interjected, her tone instantly filled with deep apologetic emotion. 'We're so sorry,' her mother sobbed. 'For everything.'

At the sound of her mother's tears Honey felt a few slide down her own cheeks and soon those few turned into a few more. By the time her father came on the line, Honey was crying. Thankfully, Edward hugged her close, pulling a handkerchief from his pocket and dabbing at her tears. 'I'm proud of you,' he whispered.

'Thank you,' she mouthed, then smiled.

On Friday morning, Woody surprised Honey by arriving in town unannounced. Edward's first indication of the event was when he heard Honey's squeal of delight. He'd just come out of the shower and was wearing a pair of denim jeans with a white towel around his shoulders, rubbing at his hair. He'd rushed to the front window, his heart pounding beneath his chest, fearful something bad had happened to the woman who seemed to constantly be on his mind. As he watched, he saw Honey literally launch herself into her brother's arms.

The resemblance between the siblings was clear, even though Woody was a good foot and a half taller than his big sister. Edward's heart rate started to settle to its normal rhythm, pounding out a beat just for Honey. She was dressed in another pair of colourful pyjama bottoms and a tight-fitting singlet top, a long open cardigan hanging down to her knees as though she'd just thrown it on at the last minute.

Woody whipped her up and whizzed her around as though she were about five years old, Honey giggling with delight. The sound washed over him and he closed his eyes, wanting to savour the moment. There was no denying the strong feelings he had for her. Not any more. She was rarely far from his thoughts and he found himself almost desperate to contrive reasons to be in her presence. When he was there, when he was close to her, breathing in her hypnotic scent, trying not to stare into her beautiful eyes, he found it difficult to restrain himself from touching her, from taking her hand and hauling her into his arms. He wanted her body pressed as close to his as physically possible. Even thinking about it now made his heart ache for her.

She was *in* him. He had no idea how it had happened but his heart had connected with hers and he had no idea what to do about it. When he'd been with Amelia, he'd always been completely in control of his emotions. Not so with Honey. Even as he watched her now, his head and heart seemed to be warring with each other. One telling him she was the only woman for him, the other saying they had too many differences to overcome.

Honey wanted children, was almost desperate to have 'a whole gaggle' of them. Edward frowned as he started to wonder *why* Honey was so vehement in her need. What was it that had made this simple desire to reproduce such a necessity within her life? He recalled the way she'd stabbed her finger at the table, saying that no child of hers would be made to feel lonely and unwanted.

Perhaps her need stemmed from wanting to show her parents how they should have raised her and Woody? To let them see that children didn't necessarily want freedom, or to be left to their own devices, they wanted to be *valued* by their parents. She was trying to right past wrongs, wrongs that had been done to her.

Both of them had had responsibilities thrust upon them and both of them had assumed control. In that way they were the same but where Honey was desperate for children, Edward knew the thought of reproducing still scared him. His parents had had five children—and then his mother and father had died. They hadn't meant to. He'd always known it had been an accident but what if…what if he *did* have children and then something bad happened to him? Some freak accident that took his life and left his children—?

'Eddie?'

Edward was startled from his reverie to see Honey waving at him from the driveway, her other arm around her brother's waist. It was then he realised he was still standing at the window, watching them but not really seeing them as his thoughts had drifted off.

'Come and meet my brother,' she called, beckoning for him to come down. Knowing it was futile to attempt to argue with Honey, he did as she bid, mindful to pull on a T-shirt before heading downstairs.

Edward invited them inside, all of them walking into the kitchen where Edward instantly put on the coffee machine. 'Cuppa?'

'Uh…have you got any herbal tea? I've been living on coffee for the past few hours to keep me awake.'

'I have some at the coach house,' Honey said instantly, and headed for the door.

'It's OK, Honey,' Edward said quickly, and produced

a box of the same type of herbal tea she had at the clinic. 'I bought some.'

Honey's eyes widened. 'You drink herbal tea now?'

Edward shrugged. 'Well, no. Not necessarily but *you* do and you're here for dinner on a regular basis and so I thought that—' He broke off as Honey put her arms around him, hugging him close.

'You're wonderful,' she told him. 'Thank you.'

Edward looked down into her face, once again struck by the mesmerising colour of her eyes. He liked it when she wore her different coloured contacts but he much preferred her natural colour. He placed his free hand in the small of her back, delighted she had appreciated his gesture of buying the tea. 'You're most welcome,' he murmured, his gaze dipping to encompass her mouth before flicking back to meet her gaze.

'Herbal tea it is, then,' Woody remarked, rubbing his hands together. Honey and Edward looked at him as though they'd forgotten he was in the room. Woody winked at his sister as she released Edward from her arms and crossed back to his side.

'So, Woody.' Edward turned his attention back to filling the kettle and switching it on. 'Honey mentioned you've worked in Tarparnii?'

'That's right. I'm due to go back in another fortnight so figured it was the perfect time to come and see my sister and check out the area she swears she's fallen in love with. I have to admit,' he said, draping his arm around Honey's shoulders, 'it is quite beautiful around here.'

'I told you so,' she said with a wide smile.

'Yeah, you did.' Woody let go of Honey and picked up the duffle bag he'd brought in with him, before holding Edward's gaze. 'My sister only picks the best.'

Edward froze for a moment, unsure whether Woody

was referring to the town of Oodnaminaby or to him. Honey had said she was very close to her brother but how much had she told him? Had she told Woody about the kisses they'd shared? The long talks they'd enjoyed? Edward swallowed, trying to read Woody's expression, but all he saw was open joviality.

'So, sis, why don't you show me the coach house and I can dump my stuff while we wait for the kettle to boil?' Woody suggested.

'You're going to stay in the coach house with Honey? Where will you sleep?' Edward looked at the tall man's stature. 'You won't fit on the couch.'

Woody chuckled. 'In Tarparnii we sleep on the floor,' he stated. 'I'll be fine.'

Edward looked at Honey for a moment before shaking his head. 'No, it's ridiculous for Woody to sleep on the floor when I have plenty of spare rooms here. You're more than welcome to stay in the house. Hamilton will be glad of the extra company,' he stated as the teenager came down the stairs and into the room, still half-asleep.

'Hey, man.' Hamilton blearily shook hands with Woody.

'OK,' Woody accepted. 'If it's no trouble, that would be great.' He looked at Honey who nodded and smiled, delighted that her brother and the man who had become so vitally important to her life were getting along well.

That evening they shared dinner with the rest of Edward's extended family. BJ brought Lorelai and baby Hannah over, whilst Peter, Annabelle and their children came to town for the night. Hamilton was in his element having so many people around and Edward and Honey quickly cobbled together enough food to feed everyone.

'Woody seems to fit right in,' Edward remarked as the two of them carried plates to the kitchen, Edward starting to stack the dishwasher.

'He's a very easygoing man. He always has been. Even when things don't work out as he plans, he seems to somehow pick himself up and soldier on. Woody recently suffered a great personal tragedy.' There was sadness behind Honey's eyes and Edward instantly found himself drawing her into his arms. She was about to say more but Edward quickly dipped his head and brushed his lips across hers.

'I'm sure he learned his excellent coping skills from his big sister. Where you felt abandoned by your parents, he didn't experience that sensation because he always had you to fill the void they left. We're the same like that, Honey. We've both worked hard to spare our younger siblings from feeling the same painful and lonely sensations we had to experience.'

'We're amazing,' she whispered as his mouth touched hers again.

'Oh, really?' Lorelai said as she walked into the room, Honey and Edward taking their time easing apart. 'You two have progressed to this stage already?'

Honey shrugged. 'Whatever "this stage" means, I guess we have.' She smiled as Edward winked at her. It was as though both of them knew their hearts had connected but neither were sure how to move forward from there.

Honey relieved Lorelai of the plates she was holding. Edward watched the two women as they chatted and laughed, moving around his kitchen, both of them feeling equally at home. Honey seemed to fit neatly into his life. Before they'd met he hadn't realised anything was missing but now, when he thought of his life without her, there seemed to be a large gaping hole filled with pain and loneliness.

Honey had experienced the same pain and loneliness as a child and there was no way he wanted either of them to feel that way ever again. Yet to discuss a future with her felt strange. Where children were concerned, they were at opposites. Slowly, though, an idea started to form in his mind. It was a plan that might help Honey to reconcile with her parents, to get her whole family back. Perhaps it would help her realise that her almost obsessive need to have children stemmed from the lack of control she'd had during her growing years. There was no way he could ever bring his own parents back but thanks to Honey he'd been able to finally make peace with their passing.

The least he could do was to support her while she took the next steps towards finding true happiness—and it was happiness he wanted to share.

# CHAPTER TEN

'Where are we going?'

Honey was standing beside her car, an overnight bag in her hand, the crispness of the April morning making itself known. Edward took the bag from her hand and stowed it in the boot.

'Have you got the keys?' he asked as Woody walked out the back door of the house, sipping a cup of coffee. Her brother had been there for a week, fitting right in with the entire town and community. He'd been invited out for dinner almost every night and Honey was pleased he was being made to feel so welcome. He was more than happy to hang around for a few more days, delighted to be filling in for her and Edward at the clinic for the next two days. Edward had planned it all and she'd often caught the two most important men in her life chatting quietly, stopping as soon as she walked into the room.

'Almost ready to go?' Woody asked, taking a sip from his mug.

'Just about.'

'Where are we going?' Honey asked for the umpteenth time, spreading her arms wide.

'I've told you,' Edward replied as he opened the driver's side door for her. 'You and I are heading out of town for the night. Woody will hold down the fort at the clinic and can always call on Lorelai if he needs support. You were right, Honey. I don't take enough time out for myself, so now I'm going to rectify that matter.'

'But I'm going with you. That's not being alone, Edward.'

He stepped forward, sliding one arm about her waist and drawing her close for a quick, soft, body-melting kiss. 'I'm not going anywhere without you,' he whispered against her lips. 'Now, in you hop.' He stepped back. 'We're taking your car and you're driving.'

'But…where?'

Edward winked at her. 'That's for me to know and for you to find out!'

'Having fun?' he asked, looking over at her from the driver's seat, the two of them happy to share the driving. They'd been on the road now for just over six hours, having stopped here and there to admire the beautiful scenery they were driving through. Edward had been thoughtful in packing food and drink for them, allowing Honey more time to stop and browse through some of the craft and antique shops they'd passed along the way.

'Having great fun. I can't believe the bargains I've managed to get.'

'I can't imagine how these stores can claim they sell antiques. More like unwanted odds and sods no one else wants.'

'Except me.'

Edward glanced at the odd mix of packages wrapped in newspaper in the back seat and smiled. 'Except you,' he agreed.

'You have to admit, those sterling-silver sugar tongs I found were an absolute steal.'

He laughed. 'A steal for whom?' He reached over and

took her hand in his, bringing it to his lips. 'You're unique, Honeysuckle. I like that about you.'

'Good.' Honey swallowed and smiled at him. 'I like it that you like that about me.'

'Even though you know where I've tricked you into coming today?' He set her hand back onto her lap and slowed the car down as they hit the outskirts of Rosedale.

'You didn't trick me, Eddie, and it didn't take me long to figure things out. You and Woody conspiring together was a pretty strong give-away.'

'You don't mind, then? Seeing your parents, I mean?'

Honey breathed out slowly. 'I'm nervous, I'm scared, I'm…nervous and scared. Oh, wait, did I already say that? See how nervous and scared I am?' She tried to laugh but it came off more as a sigh. 'It's time. It was time for me to call them and it's time for me to see them.'

'And I'll be there, beside you, the whole way,' he remarked. He slowed the car even more and flicked on the indicator to turn, driving them towards the location Woody had provided. It was the site of La Trobe Valley coal-powered electricity-generating plant. A group of protesters were starting to pack up their equipment as the sun was setting.

Edward parked the car and came around to Honey's side, opening the door and holding out his hand to her. She stood and he instantly pulled her close. 'Are you all right?' he asked. 'You're looking a bit pale.'

Honey breathed out slowly. 'It's good. I'm fine. Just stay close.'

He kissed her. 'I wouldn't be anywhere else except by your side.' It was as he said the words that he realised just how much he meant them, not only for now but for ever. The thought didn't scare him as much as he had thought it might.

They turned and headed towards the protesters. Honey stopped for a moment and shook her head. 'They're not here.'

'What?' Edward looked around.

'That's their Kombi,' she said, pointing at the circa 1960s van that had most certainly seen better days. 'But I don't see them.'

'Who are you looking for?' one of the other protesters asked, having overheard them.

'Uh...Star and Red Moon-Pie?' she asked the thin woman who was dressed in a similar tie-dyed outfit to one Edward had once seen Honey wear.

'Oh, they're in the local lock-up,' the woman responded calmly. 'Things became a little heated earlier on and the police came out and, well, if you know Red, you'll know that when the police come, it's like a red flag to a bull.'

Honey nodded. 'I know him far too well,' she responded, shaking her head. 'Thanks,' she said, and turned around, taking Edward with her as they headed back to her car. 'Typical Dad.'

'Does that upset you?' Edward asked as he slipped back behind the wheel.

Honey thought for a moment. 'Actually, no. I'm not annoyed either, just...mildly amused that in all this time my dad hasn't changed. His values and beliefs are obviously still as strong as they've always been and you know what? That's a good thing.'

'Sounds like you.'

'Really?' Honey had never thought she was like either of her parents before.

'You have firm beliefs and values, Honey, and you live them every day. You're an amazing doctor and it's clear you care for all your patients. You're smart, as has been proved by the numerous degrees you hold, and you're incredibly giving.' He turned in his seat, reaching out to cup her face in his hands. 'So very giving,' he murmured, and leaned over to kiss her.

Honey allowed herself to be swept away by his words, by his touch and by the glorious feel of his mouth on hers. She gave all of herself to him for in that one moment she knew for certain that she loved him. She had no idea what was going to happen in the future, whether or not he'd change his mind about wanting children, but right at this moment she didn't care if they never had children so long as she could stay with him for ever.

He broke off the kiss, leaning his forehead against hers as their breathing slowly started to return to normal. 'Shall we go to the police station and find out what's going on?'

Honey smiled and nodded. 'You sure know how to show a girl a good time, Dr Goldmark.'

So Honey's first sight of her parents, after eight years, was as they were brought out from the back room at the small police station. She gripped Edward's hand and was rewarded with a slight squeeze. 'I'm here,' he whispered near her ear, and when her parents stood before her, Honey found the anger she'd carried towards them simply drain out of her.

Edward was there. He was with her. Holding onto her. Keeping her grounded, keeping her safe from harm. With him by her side, she realised suddenly that she didn't need to worry about anything. The past was gone and she could do nothing to change it. The future was unwritten and anything could happen.

'Honeysuckle!' It was her father who spoke. 'That's my girl. Coming to pick up her oldies. The last time you did this was...' Red stopped and scratched his almost balding head. He looked older, so much older than Honey had realised. Her doctor's brain immediately looked for signs of sickness but found none. He'd just grown older. Her mother, at almost sixty years of age, looked incredible. Her long silvery hair, which had once been a honey blonde like her daughter's, was pulled back into a ponytail and her blue-green eyes shone with happiness.

'Woody's eighteenth birthday,' Honey remarked. 'I came home for his celebration to find both of you had managed to get yourself arrested.'

'Woody understood, Honeysuckle,' her mother began, edging slowly forward.

'He may have but I didn't.' Where Honey had always thought there would be anger when she finally told her parents how she truly felt, there was only sadness. 'Even as an adult, I didn't understand how you could leave your own children to go and attend protest rallies instead of spending time with us. You've always been fighting hard to win everyone else's battles. Why didn't you fight to win mine? Why didn't you break down the walls I was putting up when I was younger?' Tears started to prick at her eyes. 'Why weren't you there for *me* when I needed you?' Tears ran down her face and she sniffed.

'Oh, Honeysuckle,' her mother said, and within another moment she had covered the distance between them, putting her arms around her daughter, both women crying tears of healing. 'We're sorry, Honeysuckle. So sorry. We had no idea until years later how much pressure we put on you.'

'You were always so competent, so strong and so determined to do things your way, there was no persuading you otherwise,' her father added, coming over to place a hand on his daughter's back. 'Stubborn and pig-headed. Just like your old man. Nurturing and powerful, just like your beautiful mother,' Red continued.

Honey sniffed and laughed at her father's words, wiping

at the tears with her free hand, her other still firmly hold-ing onto Edward. Star backed away and pulled a handker-chief from her pocket, dabbing at her eyes and blowing her nose. Red slipped his arm about his wife's shoulders and Honey took a good long look at her parents. After forty years together, they appeared still very much in love, very much in tune with each other. She looked at Edward. Her rock, her grounding force who had stood firm through-out this ordeal, showing her just how much he supported her. Honey knew she'd do anything for him, follow him to the ends of the earth, give up on her dream of children if he asked her.

Was this how her mother had felt when she'd met Red? Was this why she'd left home, defied her parents' wishes, headed off to live her life her way? Wasn't that exactly what Honey had done all those years ago when she'd walked out of the commune? Wasn't that what she was doing now, standing here with Edward by her side? Living her life her way?

'Now,' Red said, after blowing his own nose, 'aren't you going to introduce your ol' dad to this young whip-persnapper who seems to have glued his hand to yours?'

Honey laughed and turned to introduce Edward, who suggested they all go out for dinner. Where Honey's par-ents had previously refused to eat in any restaurant given the food often had additives, they welcomed the oppor-tunity to visit the local tavern.

'Food has certainly come a long way in the past de-cade,' Star remarked as they looked at menus. 'Most places cater to different diets,' she continued, as though able to read her daughter's thoughts. Afterwards, they all piled into Honey's tiny car and drove back to her parents' van.

Her parents booked into the local caravan park, invit-ing Honey and Edward to stay with them.

'I hadn't planned on camping,' Edward remarked after they'd pitched the tent beside the van. Honey had used the foot-pump to blow up a large air mattress and unrolled the old sleeping bags her parents had provided them with.

'It's going to be wonderful,' she said with a giggle as she lay down. 'I haven't slept in a tent in well over a decade.' She stretched out her hand to him and after he'd taken off his shoes he lay down beside her.

Honey gazed into his eyes and sighed. 'Thank you, Eddie.'

'It was my pleasure.' He stroked her face, his fingers soft and gentle on her perfect skin. 'You are...exquisite,' he murmured, and a fraction of a second later she felt his mouth on hers.

Sighing into the kiss, she slid one arm around his neck, wanting to keep his head right where it was, desperate to memorise every minute emotion he evoked within her. She didn't hold back this time and put everything into the kiss. She had absolute faith that one day she and Edward would be together but until that day came she was determined to let him know just how important he was to her.

After a brief moment he deepened the kiss, slipping his tongue between her lips, amazed at how perfect she felt, how seamlessly they meshed as though they'd been made for each other. As he continued to plunder and probe the depths of her luscious mouth, Edward was pleased when she matched his hunger and need. This woman, this wild, vivacious woman made him feel as though he were the most fortunate man on the face of the earth. There was no way he would ever knowingly hurt her, his need to honour and protect her paramount.

No other woman had ever made him feel the way Honey could and that in itself was enormous for him. As much as he wanted to stay right where he was, as much as he wanted the emotions she evoked in him to take their natural course, they both knew now was not the right time. There were still a few things they had to address, namely if they *were* to get married, how were they going to solve the issue of children?

When they pulled apart, rapidly drawing breath, Honey leaned her head against his chest, secretly delighted at the fierce pounding of his heart. They lay there for a while, his arms around her as she snuggled into his chest, both seemingly content.

A few hours later, Edward woke to find he had little to no feeling in his arm and on trying to sit up rapidly remembered he was lying in a tent with Honey in his arms. They'd fallen asleep.

Carefully, he slid his arm from beneath her neck and quickly unzipped the sleeping bags, pulling them over her. When he returned to her side, she was still sound asleep but snuggled into him again.

'Mmm, Eddie,' she murmured, then slipped back into slumberland.

She was dreaming about him? A slow smile spread over Edward's face as he put an arm around her, the other one beneath his head. He closed his eyes, amazed to find that right at this moment he was incredibly content.

It was a little before four o'clock the following afternoon when they pulled Honey's car into Edward's driveway.

'That was a good trip,' she said as they headed into the house. 'And my parents have promised to come and visit on their way back to Queensland.'

Edward nodded. 'It's great. They're more than welcome to stay here.'

'That's so sweet of you,' she said, leaning up to kiss

him. He opened the back door for her and they went inside. He dropped their bags just inside the door and pulled her quickly into his arms.

'The only problem with driving is that I can't hold you or kiss you properly,' he remarked, and was just about to lower his head when both of them heard the distinct sound of a baby murmuring happily.

They frowned at each other and then looked through the kitchen into the lounge room, where the sound had come from. Quickly, they followed the noise, Edward's eyebrows shooting upwards when he found his youngest brother sitting in a comfortable chair, Hannah in his arms, giving the baby a bottle.

'Hamilton?' Edward was stunned.

'Shh. Not so loud, bro. She's almost on her way to beddy-bye land.'

Honey and Edward came quietly into the room. 'Where's Lore? Woody? Where is everyone?' Edward asked softly.

'Emergency. The details are on the table over there.' He indicated a piece of paper on the coffee table. 'Woody said for you two to come as soon as you got home if I hadn't heard from him, and I haven't heard from him.'

Honey picked up the piece of paper and read what was written in her brother's usually illegible scrawl.

'OK, but where's Lorelai?' Edward persisted. 'Why are you looking after Hannah?'

'Lorelai had an appointment at the solicitors in Tumut and was pretty worked up about it so BJ offered to drive her and Woody said he'd stay with Hannah but when the emergency call came through, Woody wasn't sure what to do so I volunteered for Hannah duty.' Hamilton spoke softly but with an adult confidence Edward had never heard before.

Hamilton took the bottle out of Hannah's mouth when she'd finished, the little baby snuggling contentedly into him. 'Go. I'll be fine here.'

'Ham. You don't know how to—'

'I know how to do a lot of things, bro. Besides, I consider Hannah my niece, my family. And if there's one thing we Goldmarks know how to do, it's to take care of our family. You taught me that, bro. Now go!' Hamilton smiled. 'Ha. Go, bro. Man, I'm funny.'

Honey had her phone out and was trying to ring Woody. 'I can't get through but he's written down that the accident is on the road between here and Tumut.'

Edward nodded and pulled Honey's car keys from his pocket. 'Let me get my medical bag.'

Within a matter of minutes they were back on the road, heading towards Tumut. Given the cellphone reception was a bit hit and miss in these parts of the mountains, Honey tried Lorelai's and BJ's phones as well as Woody's but to no avail. Ten minutes later she was finally able to get hold of her brother.

'Woody! Thank goodness. What's going on?' she asked. 'Hang on. I'm going to put you on loudspeaker so Eddie can hear what you're saying, too.'

'Oh, Honey, I'm glad to hear your voice. Are you on your way?'

'We're about fifteen kilometres out of Tumut.'

'Then you can't be too far away. Listen, a car has crashed through the safety barrier and gone off the road. One man is trapped and a woman was thrown clear. They're about to take the woman to Tumut for possible airlift to Canberra. Lorelai is here with BJ, running the rescue side of things.' He paused. 'Edward, the man is John, Lorelai's husband. It's *his* car that went through the barrier.'

'John?' Edward repeated, astonished.

'Yes.'

'What about Lore?' Edward's tone was filled with concern and Honey noticed his face had turned ashen as his quick mind processed everything.

'She's OK. She's not hurt but she was first on the scene and called it through to me. Fire and rescue crews are here. Listen. I have to go. Get here soon and drive safe.' With that, Woody ended the call. The tension within the small car was almost palpable as both doctors mentally worked through the different scenarios they might be faced with when they arrived.

It was another five minutes before they saw the road block, traffic on the road already starting to back up. Edward slowed the car and drove on the wrong side of the road, getting as close to the accident as possible.

'Park it here,' Honey said, and Edward pulled the car up next to a fire truck, the police officer responsible for controlling the traffic having recognised Edward and waved them through the barricade. They were both out the car as soon as possible, Edward collecting his medical bag as they headed towards the crash site.

BJ, Lorelai's father, being a State Emergency Services captain and an expert at this type of retrieval, was taking charge of the situation. He saw them and inclined his head towards the embankment. Edward nodded back, understanding the silent communication. BJ wanted them down at the crash site.

They moved to where the car had broken through the road barrier. It hadn't gone far but had rolled at least once, coming to rest on the driver's side, which was now completely mangled. Fire-retardant foam had been sprayed around the car, dousing any possible spark that might cause an explosion.

As they carefully picked their way along the ground, heading towards the crash site, the rescue crews peeled away part of the passenger roof, having cut through the door and roof-post, to allow easier access to John.

Lorelai was standing beside the car, her clothes and upper arms splattered with dirt, grime and dried blood, her face dirty here and there where she'd absentmindedly wiped herself. The look of complete anguish, complete desolation on her face almost broke Edward's heart.

'Lore?' Edward walked to her side, quickly putting his bag down as Lorelai turned instantly at his voice. He drew her into his arms and held his surrogate sister close.

'Oh, Edward.' Tears instantly flooded over the barriers she'd worked hard to erect. 'Edward, it's John.' She sobbed into his shoulder. He held her for a moment, wanting to reassure and help her in any way he could, but after seeing the wreckage he wasn't sure there was much he could say.

He saw Woody come up beside him. 'Come on, Lorelai. Let me take you home,' Woody offered, putting his hand on her shoulders as she eased back from Edward's comforting arms.

'Good idea. Go on up with Woody,' he offered softly. 'Let him take you home. Honey and I will look after John.'

Lorelai sniffed and nodded, swiping at her tears with her dirty hands. 'OK.' Swallowing, she turned and allowed Woody to help her up the embankment. Edward picked up his bag and turned, expecting to find Honey standing beside him, but she'd disappeared.

'Honey?' he called.

'Hey, Edward.' A fire-rescue crew member appeared from the other side of the car, walking towards him. 'Good timing.'

'Where's Honey?'

'She's taken over from Woody. She's in the car.'

'What?' He looked at the mangled car, then back to the fireman as though he was insane. Edward carefully moved closer, desperate to see Honey, desperate to know she really was all right, that she was safe. His head started to hurt and his heart hammered wildly against his chest at the thought that anything should happen to the woman he loved.

Loved?

He'd thought that before and now, in this one moment that seemed to stand still for ever, he realised it was true. He loved Honey—and nothing else mattered.

'She's fine,' the guy continued. 'Safety first. She's in no danger.'

'No danger? She's is a car that could slip down into the lake. She might get trapped. She might drown.'

'BJ has taken care of that. The car is tethered securely at the top so there's no way it'll move unless BJ wants it to.'

Edward quickly headed around to the car, being careful not to slip on the foam. 'Honey?' he called again.

'In here. We just need to secure the ropes and then, once he's in a harness, we can cut him out,' Honey called from the inside of the vehicle. 'Oh, and I'm going to need another IV bag pretty soon.'

Edward instantly shifted his attention to the car and, more importantly, to the woman who'd stubbornly crawled inside. He peered down into it, watching for a second as Honey shimmied slowly forward, a pair of pliers in her hand.

'Honeysuckle Lilly-Pilly Goldmark, what in the name of all that's sanity are you doing in that vehicle?'

His answer was one of her sweet laughs. She hadn't missed the change of last name and wondered if Edward had even realised he'd said it. 'Oh, shush, and see if that next bag of plasma's arrived from up top yet. I did radio BJ and ask for one.'

Edward checked, seeing one of the paramedics heading down with an IV bag in his hands. 'It's on its way. What's the status?'

'John's hand is wound around the phone charger cord. I need to free it to try and get the blood flowing through his limb again.'

'How is he?'

Honey sighed and when she spoke he could hear the dejection in her tone. 'Not good, Eddie. His pulse is weak, he hasn't regained consciousness and his legs are...' She stopped. 'Where's Lorelai?'

'Gone. Woody took her home.'

'Thank goodness.'

'What were you saying about his legs?'

'They're badly crushed, Eddie.' Honey freed John's hand and quickly tried to straighten it, searching for a pulse. 'Radial pulse is still not there,' she told him, before shifting carefully around to press her fingers to John's carotid pulse.

'John? John?' She called. 'Can you hear me?'

No response.

'Report?' Edward asked.

'Carotid pulse is weakening. Pass me the penlight torch,' she instructed, and held out her hand. When he passed it to her, his fingers gently brushed hers and she felt a renewal of energy. She accepted the torch and quickly shifted so she could check John's pupils. 'No, no, no.' She checked again.

'What? What is it?'

Honey sighed and closed her eyes for a moment. 'No pulse. Pupils fixed and dilated.'

There was silence and then she felt Edward's hand reach out and touch her arm. When she turned, it was to discover he was leaning in through the side of the car.

'Call it,' he said softly.

Honey reached around and found the walkie-talkie. 'BJ?' she said, and a moment later Lorelai's father's voice crackled back.

'Honey?'

'Time of death...' she checked her watch '...sixteen fifty-seven.'

Another moment of silence. 'Copy that,' BJ replied.

Edward's heart ached and he wanted nothing more than to hold her close. To let her know that she'd done all she could, that it wasn't her fault, that life went on, that he would *never* leave her, and that whatever the future brought, they would face it together.

'Let me help you,' Edward said, and with slow, careful movements Honey made her way out of the car. Once she was out, he instantly pulled her close, holding her tight.

'Poor Lorelai,' she murmured into his neck, her arms firmly around him.

'We'll get her through. Together.' He pressed his lips to hers, reassuring himself that the woman he truly loved was really all right. 'Honey, we have so much to discuss but...first things first.' He pointed to where BJ and the rescue crews were heading down towards them.

'You two go on home. Check on Lorelai and my granddaughter,' BJ told them. 'I'll finish up here.' He clapped Edward on the shoulder. 'Thanks for telling Lore to go home. She's stubborn is my girl but she's always listened to you. You're a good man, Edward. Your parents would have been incredibly proud of you, just as I am, son.'

'He's right, you know,' Honey said an hour later, fresh from her shower, as she walked into the garden Edward's mother had loved and tended for years. Edward stood there, in the middle, just looking as the sun bounced off the different-coloured flowers and leaves. When they'd arrived back in Oodnaminaby, they'd checked in on Lorelai and Hannah, pleased when Woody had informed them that both were sleeping. Woody had offered to stay at Lorelai's for the night to monitor her. Relieved from being on Hannah duty, Hamilton had headed off to sport practice.

'Who's right?' Edward asked, pondering her question.

'BJ.' Honey slid her arms around Edward's waist, delighted when he held her close. 'Your parents would have been so proud of the man you are. The way you love and care about everyone, the way you have a calm authority that puts people at ease and gets the job done.'

'I'm just sorry they never got to meet you. My mother would have loved you.'

'Really? Most people find me a little...too flamboyant for their liking.'

'My mother loved things of beauty.'

Honey nodded. 'This garden is testimony to that.'

Edward looked down at her. '*You're* a woman of beauty, my Honeysuckle.' He breathed in deeply. 'I love your special scent, that sweet yet earthy spice that surrounds you.' He bent and kissed her left cheek. 'I love your laugh.' He kissed her right cheek. 'I love your sparkling, expressive eyes.' He kissed her eyelids closed, Honey gasping with sensual delight, her lips parting as her heart rate increased.

'I love your teasing, your verve for life, your essence.' He pressed kisses along her forehead. 'I love your smile and your plump, addictive mouth.' He brushed his lips across hers.

Honey wasn't sure she could deal with the wild pounding of her heart against her ribs, the blood thrumming through her ears with each word he spoke, with each caress he bestowed upon her as though she was the most precious person in the world.

'I love you, my Honeysuckle Lilly-Pilly.' And this time, when he claimed her lips, he deepened the kiss, letting her feel just how true his words were. A while later he pulled back and spread butterfly kisses over her face, before burrowing into her long, glorious neck, which had so often tantalised him. Now he was free to kiss her skin whenever he wanted, free to touch her, to gather her close and declare to the world that *this* was the woman for him.

Honey settled herself in his arms and sighed. 'Look at the sun. Almost down. Still radiant and breath-taking.'

He caressed her loose hair, delighted with the different colours sifting through his fingers as though making their own enchanting sunset. 'Yes.' He looked down into her face, his eyes alive with happiness. 'Just like you—chasing away my greys and bringing colour into my life. Breath-taking.' He gasped as she leaned up and nipped his lower lip with her teeth. 'Literally breath-taking,' he said with a laugh, and kissed her again.

'Honey, you make me happy. I want to travel with you, I want to share new experiences with you, I want to be with you for the rest of my life. I don't care where I am or what we're doing, so long as we're doing it together.'

'And children?' Honey swallowed. 'Do you want to have children?' She held her breath, knowing this was a big question for Edward to answer. A moment later, when he didn't immediately jump in, she continued, 'I've been thinking about why you might not want to have any and, honestly, Edward, I don't think it's because you've "done your time", so to speak. I think it's because you're worried that if we have children and something happens to us, our children would be left alone—just as you were.'

'Accidents happen.' He nodded then shrugged. 'Having children means pressure and responsibility. What if something *does* happen, Honey? Then our children will be subjected to all the painful emotions I've lived with for the past eight years.'

'Then we'll do whatever we can to make it easier for them. We'll put counter-measures in place, just as your parents did.' When he frowned at her she smiled and leaned up to kiss his forehead. 'On my first day here you told me you'd had help in raising your younger brothers. Not only did you have Peter and Bart to lean on but you had BJ and Lorelai and the majority of the people in this community. Your parents provided you with the best back-up plan. They cared about you and your brothers and I'll bet they're looking down from heaven right now, incredibly proud of you.' She nodded. 'We don't have to have children straight away, Eddie. I still want to have one or two—'

'Not a whole gaggle?'

Honey smiled and shook her head. 'Seeing my parents again, talking with them, opening up has been good for me, which is probably the reason why you took me to see them. You realised, didn't you, that through my vehemence in wanting children, I was hoping to right the wrongs done to me?' She shrugged one shoulder. 'That's not a good reason to have children. We should have children because it's what we both want, deep down in our hearts. And I know, for a fact, that we will make excellent parents given we've practically raised our siblings and they've turned out pretty fantastic.'

'You don't want to have kids straight away?' he checked again.

'No. I want to have some time with just you and me. Together. Figuring out who we are as a couple. Besides,

I'm young enough to wait a while. I am only seven and a quarter, you know.'

Edward's smile was bright as he leaned forward and kissed her glorious mouth.

'I love you, Edward Austin Goldmark,' she murmured against his mouth. 'I've always been looking for the place I belonged and I had hoped that Oodnaminaby might be that place…but I was wrong.'

'You were?'

'*You* are the place where I belong.'

'Home is where the heart is,' he recited, and she nodded.

'So long as we're together.'

'Together.'

'Home is where the heart is and my heart belongs to you.'

Edward nodded, then spun her from his arms but still held onto her hand. 'Come with me. I have a present for you.'

'Really? A present?'

'I saw it on the table by the front door when we arrived back this afternoon but with the accident and all, I temporarily forgot.' She allowed him to lead her into his home, the walls feeling as though they were singing with delight. The house would once more be a home, home to two people who loved each other with all their hearts.

'Go and sit down. I'll be there in a moment.'

'Ooh.' Honey clapped her hands together, delighted excitement filling her. She did as she was told and a moment later he came into the room, stopping by the armchair she sat in, going down on bended knee in front of her. Honey's eyes grew as wide as saucers. 'Edward?'

'Honeysuckle,' he began, and took her hands in his, a long, thin rectangular box by his side. 'I saw these ad-

vertised in a medical journal and I knew I had to get one
for you. It's right and I hope it shows you just how much
I not only love you but appreciate you. You're a unique
woman and therefore you require a unique gift.'

He picked up the box and placed it in her hands. 'Honey,
I love you. I want you with me always and I hope you'll
accept this as a token of my undying love.'

'Is that a proposal?' she asked.

'It is.'

'Of marriage?'

'Yes.'

'Good. Just wanted to make sure,' she said with a nervous laugh. She couldn't believe how badly her hands
were trembling but it was curiosity that moved her forward. She removed the ribbon, then the paper. Finally,
she lifted the lid on the box, pushed back the white tissue paper and gasped, covering her mouth with both her
hands as she looked at what he'd bought her.

'Oh, Eddie.' Her eyes filled with tears. 'Really?' She
looked at him and he nodded.

'Really.'

Honey looked back down at her gift, unable to believe
the thin rectangular plaque that read, Dr Honeysuckle
Goldmark General Practitioner and then had a list of her
degrees underneath.

'You bought me a plaque of my very own. I've always
wanted one.'

'I know. I remember you telling me. I've already con-
tacted my solicitor to draw up the papers to make you
an official partner in the Oodnaminaby Family Medical
Practice. You belong in this town. It's your home…your
home with me.'

Honey ran her fingers lovingly over the lettering before
leaning forward to cup his face in her hands and kiss his

gorgeous mouth. 'Honeysuckle Goldmark. I love it. This is the most *perfect* gift you could ever have given me. A place to belong. A place to call home. A place in your heart.'

'Is that you accepting my proposal?' he asked with a twinkle in his eyes.

'Yes, it is.'

'Good. Just wanted to make sure.'

With that, Edward stood and lifted the plaque from her lap before pulling her up and into his arms, kissing the woman of his dreams with all the love in his heart.

\* \* \* \* \*

*Mills & Boon® Hardback*

*January 2012*

# ROMANCE

| | |
|---|---|
| **The Man Who Risked It All** | Michelle Reid |
| **The Sheikh's Undoing** | Sharon Kendrick |
| **The End of her Innocence** | Sara Craven |
| **The Talk of Hollywood** | Carole Mortimer |
| **Secrets of Castillo del Arco** | Trish Morey |
| **Hajar's Hidden Legacy** | Maisey Yates |
| **Untouched by His Diamonds** | Lucy Ellis |
| **The Secret Sinclair** | Cathy Williams |
| **First Time Lucky?** | Natalie Anderson |
| **Say It With Diamonds** | Lucy King |
| **Master of the Outback** | Margaret Way |
| **The Reluctant Princess** | Raye Morgan |
| **Daring to Date the Boss** | Barbara Wallace |
| **Their Miracle Twins** | Nikki Logan |
| **Runaway Bride** | Barbara Hannay |
| **We'll Always Have Paris** | Jessica Hart |
| **Heart Surgeon, Hero...Husband?** | Susan Carlisle |
| **Doctor's Guide to Dating in the Jungle** | Tina Beckett |

# HISTORICAL

| | |
|---|---|
| **The Mysterious Lord Marlowe** | Anne Herries |
| **Marrying the Royal Marine** | Carla Kelly |
| **A Most Unladylike Adventure** | Elizabeth Beacon |
| **Seduced by Her Highland Warrior** | Michelle Willingham |

# MEDICAL

| | |
|---|---|
| **The Boss She Can't Resist** | Lucy Clark |
| **Dr Langley: Protector or Playboy?** | Joanna Neil |
| **Daredevil and Dr Kate** | Leah Martyn |
| **Spring Proposal in Swallowbrook** | Abigail Gordon |

*Mills & Boon® Large Print*

*January 2012*

# ROMANCE

| | |
|---|---|
| **The Kanellis Scandal** | Michelle Reid |
| **Monarch of the Sands** | Sharon Kendrick |
| **One Night in the Orient** | Robyn Donald |
| **His Poor Little Rich Girl** | Melanie Milburne |
| **From Daredevil to Devoted Daddy** | Barbara McMahon |
| **Little Cowgirl Needs a Mum** | Patricia Thayer |
| **To Wed a Rancher** | Myrna Mackenzie |
| **The Secret Princess** | Jessica Hart |

# HISTORICAL

| | |
|---|---|
| **Seduced by the Scoundrel** | Louise Allen |
| **Unmasking the Duke's Mistress** | Margaret McPhee |
| **To Catch a Husband...** | Sarah Mallory |
| **The Highlander's Redemption** | Marguerite Kaye |

# MEDICAL

| | |
|---|---|
| **The Playboy of Harley Street** | Anne Fraser |
| **Doctor on the Red Carpet** | Anne Fraser |
| **Just One Last Night...** | Amy Andrews |
| **Suddenly Single Sophie** | Leonie Knight |
| **The Doctor & the Runaway Heiress** | Marion Lennox |
| **The Surgeon She Never Forgot** | Melanie Milburne |

# Mills & Boon® Hardback
## February 2012

# ROMANCE

| | |
|---|---|
| **An Offer She Can't Refuse** | Emma Darcy |
| **An Indecent Proposition** | Carol Marinelli |
| **A Night of Living Dangerously** | Jennie Lucas |
| **A Devilishly Dark Deal** | Maggie Cox |
| **Marriage Behind the Façade** | Lynn Raye Harris |
| **Forbidden to His Touch** | Natasha Tate |
| **Back in the Lion's Den** | Elizabeth Power |
| **Running From the Storm** | Lee Wilkinson |
| **Innocent 'til Proven Otherwise** | Amy Andrews |
| **Dancing with Danger** | Fiona Harper |
| **The Cop, the Puppy and Me** | Cara Colter |
| **Back in the Soldier's Arms** | Soraya Lane |
| **Invitation to the Prince's Palace** | Jennie Adams |
| **Miss Prim and the Billionaire** | Lucy Gordon |
| **The Shameless Life of Ruiz Acosta** | Susan Stephens |
| **Who Wants To Marry a Millionaire?** | Nicola Marsh |
| **Sydney Harbour Hospital: Lily's Scandal** | Marion Lennox |
| **Sydney Harbour Hospital: Zoe's Baby** | Alison Roberts |

# HISTORICAL

| | |
|---|---|
| **The Scandalous Lord Lanchester** | Anne Herries |
| **His Compromised Countess** | Deborah Hale |
| **Destitute On His Doorstep** | Helen Dickson |
| **The Dragon and the Pearl** | Jeannie Lin |

# MEDICAL

| | |
|---|---|
| **Gina's Little Secret** | Jennifer Taylor |
| **Taming the Lone Doc's Heart** | Lucy Clark |
| **The Runaway Nurse** | Dianne Drake |
| **The Baby Who Saved Dr Cynical** | Connie Cox |

*Mills & Boon® Large Print*

*February 2012*

# ROMANCE

| | |
|---|---|
| **The Most Coveted Prize** | Penny Jordan |
| **The Costarella Conquest** | Emma Darcy |
| **The Night that Changed Everything** | Anne McAllister |
| **Craving the Forbidden** | India Grey |
| **Her Italian Soldier** | Rebecca Winters |
| **The Lonesome Rancher** | Patricia Thayer |
| **Nikki and the Lone Wolf** | Marion Lennox |
| **Mardie and the City Surgeon** | Marion Lennox |

# HISTORICAL

| | |
|---|---|
| **Married to a Stranger** | Louise Allen |
| **A Dark and Brooding Gentleman** | Margaret McPhee |
| **Seducing Miss Lockwood** | Helen Dickson |
| **The Highlander's Return** | Marguerite Kaye |

# MEDICAL

| | |
|---|---|
| **The Doctor's Reason to Stay** | Dianne Drake |
| **Career Girl in the Country** | Fiona Lowe |
| **Wedding on the Baby Ward** | Lucy Clark |
| **Special Care Baby Miracle** | Lucy Clark |
| **The Tortured Rebel** | Alison Roberts |
| **Dating Dr Delicious** | Laura Iding |

0112 GEN STD LP